BISHOP'S BRIDE

SEVEN BRIDES FOR SEVEN BROTHERS
BOOK FIVE

KATHLEEN LAWLESS

ISBN ebook: 978-1-9990635-1-1

ISBN print: 978-1-989873-54-0

Dedication

Dedicated to John, the love of my life. My alpha male hero.

CHAPTER 1

Rose leaned over and stroked the cheek of baby Charlotte, nestled against Georgina, owner of the local café and more recently her employer. How could a newborn's skin be so impossibly soft?

She straightened and looked around as the newly-built women's institute hall in Bullet filled up with wedding guests. It was hard to believe she was here in this town. If only her sister Lily was with her.

The air was heavy with the fragrance of hundreds of colorful flowers, the likes of which Rose had never seen before. At the front of the hall the seven handsome Mason brothers stood in a somber line flanking the groom. Rose's gaze centered on Bishop standing next to his twin brother.

Rose was here for only one reason. To find her sister. And while they didn't know it yet, the twins were slated to be her number one accomplices in that goal.

She stood along with everyone else as the background music abruptly changed in tempo. Most heads turned toward the back of the hall where the bridesmaids, including the baby's mother Laura, led the bridal procession. Rose never took her eyes off Bishop.

"ROSE IS WATCHING YOU LIKE A HAWK." Bishop's twin brother, Barron, leaned over and spoke directly in his ear.

"Bad choice of words." Bishop replied, low-voiced, from the corner of his mouth.

"You're right. Really bad."

Bishop's gaze slid past the blond in question who was seated next to Georgina. She was a piece of work all right. Up to no good, it would appear. He refrained from further comment as the bride glided toward where Blake, the groom, stood at the front of the hall. A wedding was hardly the time or the place to focus on their suspicious stowaway or their mortal enemy, Guy Hawkes, the man who had killed their brother in front of their eyes. The man whom they, along with the other Mason brothers, had sworn a blood oath to destroy.

It took very little time for the vows and rings to be exchanged, the groom to kiss his bride, and the guests in the hall to noticeably relax.

Bishop exhaled, aware he'd not been the only one on edge, as the brothers all waited to see if Hawkes would choose today to make another move against them.

"How many more of these weddings do you think there'll be?" Barron asked as the line of groomsmen disbanded.

Bishop shrugged. "Understand we got a christening up next."

"Oh, yeah," Barron said. "Brody and Laura were waiting for Braydon to get back from his honeymoon." He shot his twin a cheeky grin. "Don't rightly understand why one of us wasn't slated for the role of godfather."

Bishop snorted. "Who in their right mind would want either of us to see to their young one's spiritual development?"

As Barron wandered off Bishop glanced across the room, where Rose had been watching his every move. He stayed where he was, didn't look away, and neither did she. Her dark blue eyes locked with his, and for a second he felt as if they were the only two people in the room. Which was crazy with near a hundred townsfolk mingling around, congratulating the happy couple before lining up near the beer keg or wandering about talking to other guests.

For that matter, he was feeling mighty thirsty himself.

"BULLET WOMEN'S INSTITUTE." Hawkes snorted as he glared at the shiny new hall perched on a patch of town land that should have been his. "Who the hell do these skirts think they are anyway? Showing up all fancy from the city, telling me how my town ought to be run." He spat into the dusty street, still deeply rutted with wheel marks from flooding caused by the recent monsoon.

"Shame that fire we set didn't stop 'em cold," Denim offered. "Bastards just carried on, almost as if it had never happened."

"Shut up," Hawkes said to his foreman. "Shut up and let me think."

He didn't like the way things were going with the Masons. The vermin were multiplying like rabbits, worse than the greasers. More wives, more brats, more Masons in his way. Or did the recent additions weaken the foundation?

He smiled at the realization that Brody Mason suddenly had a lot more vulnerable spots to attack.

Take now, for instance. How hard would it be to set the place on fire and bolt the doors from the outside so everyone in there roasted alive like spuds in hot coals? The thought widened his smile. Except there had been too many fires lately. He had to find a different way. At a time when he wasn't expecting the sheriff to show up.

Hawkes had Sheriff Yates handled, but you never knew when someone you trusted might come down with a sudden attack of conscience. Especially if the "accident" happened to take out half the town.

"Do you believe that foreign bitch when she says there are no pearls?" Denim asked.

Hawkes gave him a dirty look. Didn't the cur know how to hold his tongue when he was told?

"Mr. Fancy Pants is long gone," Hawkes said. "Mark my words, if there were any pearls to be found he'd still be sniffing around."

"There you are, Hawkes. Been looking everywhere for you." Sheriff Yates joined them on his tired-looking nag.

"You know how much I love a wedding," Hawkes said sarcastically. "Can't seem to stay away."

"Just got back from the office in Yuma," Yates said. "Convinced them that reporter fella musta been killed by some drifter traveling through. Did like you said and made it sound like a robbery."

Hawkes inwardly rolled his eyes. How had he come to be surrounded by a bunch of incompetents? Yates couldn't think for himself if his ass needed to be wiped. Denim wasn't any better. But at least his foreman followed instructions without asking a lot of questions. And didn't object to a little blood staining his hands from time to time.

Across the street, the hall's wide front doors were flung open. The sound of music and laughter spilled out into the afternoon, along with the smell of some damn good vittles. Hawkes's stomach rumbled.

"Go ahead and enjoy yourselves," he muttered under his breath to no one in particular. "Be the last party in this town for a good long time if I have my way."

Denim gave him a hopeful look. "Sounds like you got a plan."

Hawkes set his horse in motion, leaving Yates behind. Denim followed, ever the obedient puppet. "When don't I have a plan?"

Denim's horse fell into step alongside his. "You gonna tell me about this secret plan of yours?"

"When the time is right," Hawkes said. First his scheme needed a little fine-tuning.

BISHOP SIPPED on his beer and watched the crowd, ever vigilant, as he knew the others were as well. The only way to be as long as Hawkes walked free.

He whirled when he felt someone tap him on the shoulder and found Rose facing him. How had she snuck up on him like that? And how had she fooled him, even for a second, with that boy-garb she had been wearing when she tried to pick his pocket?

She stood nearly as tall as he did, willowy rather than curvy, but still very unmistakably female with a trim waist flaring to slightly rounded hips beneath her simple blue gown. Her honey-blond hair was pulled back from her smooth, high forehead and fell halfway down her back in soft waves. "Can I talk to you, Bishop?"

"I'm Barron," he drawled, in a deliberate attempt to discomfit her.

Her gaze on his never wavered. "No, you're not."

He blew out a breath. How was it she was the only one he couldn't put one over on? He and Barron had been confusing folks since the day they were born. The only other person who could always tell them apart was their brother Joe. Right up till the day he had been killed by Hawkes.

Rose's gaze moved over his face with a scrutiny that unnerved him, almost as if she was peeling back the skin and having a look inside at the inner workings of his brain. It was spooky. He crossed his arms over his chest. "So talk."

To his surprise, she tucked her hand through his elbow, forcing him to alter his stance. Apparently his defensive pose didn't rattle her any more than his scowl. When she began to walk, he was forced to move with her or end up looking churlish. Across the room he saw Barron smirking at him.

"I never really thanked you properly for not turning me in to the authorities the night I tried to steal your book wagon."

"Forget it," he said brusquely. "Barron and I had our share of times we could have been nabbed by the law and someone helped us. Figured it was time to pay back some good will."

"Anyway, Georgina has been very kind. In fact, everyone in Bullet has been quite lovely." She sighed in a way that Bishop couldn't help but notice her bosom heaving with the motion. "But there is one little thing I need your help with. You and your brother."

He stopped point-blank and stared down at her. Every run-in he'd had with her, Rose refused to tell him much more than her name. Along with the name of some supposedly missing sister, likely a story she'd invented in a bid for sympathy. Even when threatened with the law, she had refused to tell him why she was dressed like a boy or why she had tried to steal the book wagon. When her attempts to corral the wagon were thwarted, she'd stowed away on it.

She was stroking his arm with her free hand now, and he felt the warm pressure from her touch clear through his shirt and jacket to his skin below. Was she trying to soften him up, or was the gesture unconscious on her part?

She raised her head and smoothed back an escaped wisp of hair. "I haven't been here long but I've seen how close you are to your family. All of them. Kind of gives me hope you might understand."

"Might understand what?"

"Why I was on my own when we met up."

He'd wondered that a lot. In truth, he'd spent more time thinking about Rose than he cared to admit. But it was unusual to see a young woman alone in these parts unless she was a mail-order bride on her way to meet up with a soon-to-be husband. Most gals her age, with a year or two on twenty, in the west where men outnumbered the women by a long shot, were already married and established in their life.

"Figured you were running from someone," Bishop said. "Maybe a man who didn't treat you too good." That had been the case with Storm when Blake and she met. Happy news for Blake when he'd found out Storm was a widow. And now the two of them had been happily wed for at least an hour.

"I figure if I want your help, I owe you the truth," she said. "Is there someplace we can sit?"

Henrietta swung into the seat next to Amanda and blew out a breath. "I feel like I haven't had a spare second since I got back."

Amanda smiled at her fellow bridesmaid and sister-in-law. "Probably because you haven't. That must have been quite the trip." Shortly after their wedding, Henrietta's new husband had insisted they travel to Argentina so he could meet the family she hadn't seen in over ten years.

Henrietta nodded. "I've traveled a lot over the years, but I must say, nothing has ever felt so good as coming home to Bullet and the ranch and everyone here."

"How was your family when you showed up with Braydon?"

"It was the weirdest feeling, almost as if I had never left. My father is still an arrogant bully, with my brothers falling over themselves to gain his approval. My mother is like part of the wallpaper. It's not a very happy place." Her smile widened. "No surprise to me they loved Braydon. I heard my father refer to him as a 'man's man.' "

"I think all the Masons got tarred with that particular brush." Amanda laid a hand on her slightly rounded belly, reassured to feel a faint flutter.

Henrietta waved her hand to encompass their surroundings. "The hall looks amazing. I love what you named it."

"Tell that to some of the townsfolk. They think I'm getting a little up on myself."

"People don't like change. Speaking of change, I was sorry to see what happened to your house here in town."

Amanda shrugged. "No one was hurt in the explosion or the fire. That's the most important thing."

"I know this is not the time or the place." Henrietta's

words were punctuated by the first strains of the wedding waltz. Amid good-natured jeers and cat-calls, Blake made his way to the center of the room with Storm and took her into his arms.

"They look so good together," Amanda said.

"Those dance lessons you connived to send them on together certainly paid off. In more ways than one. Any bets on which one of the others will be next to take the plunge?"

"Until recently I would have said all bets are off. But then Rose showed up, stowed away in the back of the book wagon. And right now, there is something interesting going on between her and Bishop. You were about to say?"

"It'll keep." Henrietta got to her feet as Braydon and Bradley walked toward them. "I have an idea for the land where your house used to stand."

Braydon elbowed Bradley as they got close. "I told you the girls would be in cahoots before too long." He spoke loudly enough for Amanda and Henrietta to hear him. "You're giving your wife too much freedom," he added, his words punctuated with a grin. "Oughtn't a woman in her condition be tucked away at home, not out gallivanting at a wedding?"

Amanda rose and glided into Bradley's arms. "Never you boys mind."

Amanda saw the way Bradley made eye contact with Braydon over her head as he slipped his arm around her.

"They're all headstrong, these women of ours." Then Bradley sent her that special smile that warmed her right to her toes, as he gave her stomach the barest of affectionate pats.

Amanda sighed in contentment. Henrietta was right. There truly was no place like home.

Rose blinked hopefully up at Bishop. She'd never played the simpering, helpless female before and had no idea if she could pull it off. Growing up as she had, there'd been no opportunity to simper and languish. Pa had preached a lot of hellfire and brimstone, tempered with "spare the rod and spoil the child."

She and Lily had learned at a young age how to be careful so as to not set him off. Ma never said a word for or against, just followed along with a blind obedience that was also expected from the girls.

"There's a bench out front," Bishop said. "It'll be quieter there."

Rose looked around the large, busy room. The dance floor was getting busy. In the background food was being set out by the town ladies, with Georgina supervising. She felt a bit guilty for not being there helping, but this was more important.

"You're not needed in here?"

He gave her a cheeky grin. She bet the local girls found him irresistible, with that dimple creasing one cheek when he smiled.

"Nothing anyone can do for Blake now that he's wed."

"Some women out there feel marriage is worse than jail," she retorted.

"Some marriages likely are."

Out in front of the hall, he dusted the new bench off with his hand before she sat down and he took a seat alongside her.

"My ma," she said, before she could stop herself. Then she bit her bottom lip hard.

"Wondered if this maybe had something to do with your folks," he said.

She shook her head and swallowed before she chose her words carefully. "Not them. My sister."

"Married and in jail?" Bishop asked.

He looked younger when he flashed her that teasing smile. But she knew enough to recognize that Bishop and his twin had grown up fast and early, just like her.

Rose shook her head. "Lily was kidnapped a couple of months ago, and I've been looking for her ever since. I tracked her and her captor easy enough when they were in the brush, but I lost them once they hit civilization. Not long after that, I ran into you and Barron."

"Where are your folks?"

Rose made a face. "Praying to the Lord for Lily's safe return. And condemning my soul to hell because I set out after her."

"Your pa a preacher?"

"Worse," Rose said. "A missionary. Hell-bent on bringing salvation to the 'heathens,' as he calls the native tribes around these parts."

She didn't take to his pitying look as he spoke.

"I've met his type a time or two. Can't have been easy for you growing up around that."

Rose was having none of his pity. "Doesn't matter much when that's all you know. Moving around all the time. Keeping us girls 'pure for God.'"

"Sounds like there were no gentlemen callers," Bishop said.

Rose didn't dignify his remark with an answer. As if Pa would let any man within a hundred feet of his family.

"I'm worried about Lily," Rose said. "She's younger. Sweet.

The man who grabbed her—" Rose shuddered at the memory. "Not what anyone would call a gentleman. He and his buddies killed a helpless tribe of mostly women and children. They took off just as we got there. Pa was praying over the dead bodies when the man came back. Lily and I ran to hide, but Lily moved too slow. She tripped. Before we knew it, one of them scooped her up and rode off with her, lickety-split."

"And you went after her." Was that admiration she heard in his voice?

"She won't make it on her own. That man ..." She shuddered at the memory. "He was big and rough and dirty."

"She could already be dead," Bishop said.

Rose gave him a baleful look. That was the last thing she wanted to hear.

"Know your brother, Barron?" At his nod, she continued, "I'm willing to bet you'd do anything for him. Well, that's how I feel about Lily."

"'Fraid I can't help you, Rose. Barron and I, we got our hands full with the ranch and—" He paused. "Some other unfinished business."

Rose twisted her hands together in her lap. "I think he sold her," she blurted out. "I heard him say to the others that she'd fetch a pretty penny. Being innocent and all."

CHAPTER 2

B ishop blew out a breath before he found his way to his feet. He felt only the faintest lick of regret as he looked down at his companion and slowly shook his head. "You'd best be asking someone else."

To his dismay Rose made her way to her feet as well. He'd known from the first, what with her dressed like a boy and trying to steal the book wagon, that she was going to be trouble. Bringing her here to Bullet had been a mistake.

He knew nothing about women. Nothing about proper ladies, anyway. The whores were different. Them he understood. He was a mark, a job, nothing personal, same as when him and Barron used to run cons. Nothing was ever personal.

But seeing the way Rose looked at him, it was clear she was hell bent on making this personal. Far too damn personal for his own comfort.

"You can't tell me you don't care about your brothers!"

Bishop grunted. Put like that, it was impossible not to think about Joe being killed by Hawkes. That night marked the first time he'd realized it was no longer just him and

Barron against the evil doers. Turned out the Masons, every last one of them starting with Brody, were as invested in destroying Hawkes as the twins were.

"Well, I care about my sister every bit as much!"

"Is this a bad time?"

Bishop looked up in relief as they were joined by Barron, his twin.

Rose squared her shoulders and faced the two of them, clearly not feeling the least bit outnumbered the way she ought to. "I was telling Bishop about my sister."

Barron choked on a sip of his beer. "Don't tell me there's two of you!"

"I bet folks say that to you two all the time."

He and Barron exchanged a conspiratorial glance.

"Well, Lily and I aren't twins, and we are nothing like each other. But she's blood." Rose waved an expansive hand. "I've heard enough to know you seven aren't blood, but you're every bit as close. Maybe even more so because of that. There's no choosing your relatives," she added bitterly.

"What do you mean?" Barron clapped a hand on Bishop's shoulder. "I would always choose this guy to be on my team. Even if we didn't come from the same stock."

"I feel the same about Lily," Rose said. "It was always my job to protect her. Except for that one time I couldn't."

"Where is she now?" Barron asked.

"I don't know," Rose said. "But I figure you two, when you're driving the book wagon around, are my best chance to find her."

"How do you figure?"

"Folks in neighboring towns know the wagon. They watch for you. Good chance they'll tell you stuff they'd never tell a stranger who just happens to show up in town asking questions."

Bishop shoved his hands into his pockets. "I was telling Rose, we got our own stuff to take care of. Missing person is something to take up with the law."

Rose turned her gaze toward the street. "Three men on horseback were across the way earlier. Seemed pretty darn interested in the goings on here. One of them was that useless sheriff. So don't you all be telling me to take my problems to the law."

Bishop shot a look at Barron. "Hawkes?"

"Must have been," Barron said.

Bishop's gaze skimmed the top of Rose's head to take in the surrounding countryside. All was still. Still enough to raise the hair on the back of his neck. He berated himself for allowing Rose to distract him, even for a second. He should have spotted Hawkes himself.

As usual, Barron seemed to read his thoughts. "Don't beat yourself up. You two go in while I take a quick look around out back to make sure he's gone. I was sent by the new Mr. and Mrs. Mason to fetch you both. There's a wedding going on, in case you forgot."

"We'll wait here. Just in case," Bishop said.

Barron was back in less than a minute. "No sign of anyone." Barron held open the door for Rose to go first. Bishop followed his brother inside, relieved when Rose headed toward Georgina.

"Not like you to turn down the damsel in distress," Barron said.

Bishop flushed. Something about Rose made him want to turn and run, at the same time as he had the urge to see after her well-being. Enough to wipe that worried frown from her face once and for all.

"How do we even know her story is on the up-and-up?" Bishop said defensively. "She could be setting us up, for all we know."

"You didn't always used to be so suspicious."

"And you didn't used to always fall for every sob story that came our way."

Barron gave him a level glance. "What if it was me that got snatched? Wouldn't you do everything in your power to secure my release?"

Damn his brother!

Bishop squared his shoulders. "All I'm saying is this is not our fight."

Barron shrugged. "Just saying. All those fights we threw, folks we conned. Maybe it's come around our turn to do for someone else for a change. Like this fight with Hawkes. It's reassuring to know we're not in it alone."

"Reassuring for who?" Despite what Barron said, Bishop knew he was playing devil's advocate. Knew his twin was as impatient as he was to see Hawkes out of the picture once and for all.

Braydon interrupted. "There you both are! Henny picked up one of those new Kodak camera boxes when we were away. She wants to get a family portrait."

Reluctantly, Bishop posed along with the rest of them, feeling like a fool standing there with his face frozen in what was surely a goofy-looking smile, aware of the way Rose watched him when she thought he wasn't looking.

He'd already told her no.

Was she expecting him to change his mind just because of one sad, disappointed expression? Heck, her old man was a missionary. He was the one Rose ought to be cajoling on behalf of her sister.

Except he'd met men like that. Men who thought they were better than anyone else. Thought they held the ear of the Almighty. Believed the suffering of mere mortals was all part of God's will.

He pressed his lips together. The man couldn't be much of a father if he didn't care enough for his own daughter's safety to do more than lift his praying beads.

"What? Having a change of heart?" Barron glanced from him to Rose and back to him, a questioning look on his face.

"No!" Bishop said vehemently. Except he had felt himself start to soften. Rose was doing a good job of working him over with those eyes of hers, managing to get under his skin.

Benjamin sidled up to them and clinked his glass against theirs. "You realize we three are the last men standing."

"Bachelors," he added, at Bishop's puzzled look.

"You planning to be next?" Bishop asked.

"I don't happen to believe wedded bliss is for everyone," Ben said.

"Hear, hear to that!" Barron said.

Bishop nodded his agreement. Deliberately he turned his back on Rose. Last thing he needed was those sad, puppy-dog eyes making him feel guilty.

ROSE SAT at the table next to her employer from the café, Georgina, alongside Amanda, Laura, and Henrietta. Mostly she listened as the four of them chatted like the old friends they obviously were. She appreciated them going out of their way to include her, but not in a million years could she feel like one of them. Moving around all the time with her family, there had been no chance to form close friendships.

As she and Lily got older, it felt like it was just the two of them. Their parents would get so caught up in their missionary work that often times they'd forget about the girls for days at a time, leaving them to fend for themselves and look out for each other. Without Lily, Rose felt as if an integral part of her was missing.

"Sorry, Rose," Amanda said. "Here we've been jabbering away about things you know nothing about. It's just so exciting to have Henny back. There's lots to fill her in about since she was away."

Rose had learned Henrietta was from Argentina originally, and that she and Braydon travelled there soon after they were married. A trip of such undertaking, to a place that sounded halfway around the world, was far outside her imaginings.

"You all have known each other so long, don't mind me," she said hastily.

The women all burst into laughter at her words. What had she said that was so funny?

Laura, with baby Charlotte in her arms, leaned across the table toward her. "We weren't laughing at you. It's just that we've only known each other for less than a year. Amanda and Georgina grew up in Bullet but never socialized. And even though I grew up nearby in Yuma, I was gone for ten years. Henrietta, our globe-trotter, is relatively new to the area. Same as Storm, the bride."

"We never stayed put in any one place for long," Rose said.

Georgina gave her hand a squeeze. "Consider this home and stay for as long as you want."

Rose heaved a sigh. "I wish I could." The sense of community she had seen since her arrival was a new experience. But she'd learned not to get attached. It made moving on easier when the time came.

"Now that I'm back," Henrietta said, "and not about to

be sitting around idle, I have an idea for the land where your house used to be before it burned down, Amanda. Unless you have your own plans."

Amanda patted her stomach. "I'm already kind of busy with a few things. Besides this little project, there's still a lot that needs to be done with this hall before I take on anything else. What were you thinking?"

"I was thinking it was past time Bullet had an honest-to-goodness hotel," Henrietta said.

"Does that mean your treasure-hunting days are over?" Amanda asked.

Henrietta smiled across the room to where her handsome new husband stood alongside several of his brothers. "I found the best, most valuable treasure in the whole world right here. And not just Braydon." She beamed at her friends. "You ladies as well."

The hole in Rose's heart yawned. She had to find Lily! Maybe the two of them could eventually settle some place nice like Bullet. Make friends for the first time ever. Plan for the future.

Laura shifted her infant daughter from one arm to the other as if she'd been doing it forever. "You must come to Charlotte's christening next week, Rose. We've been waiting for Henrietta and Braydon to return so they can be godparents."

Rose found herself nodding in agreement. The christening of the tiny bundle in Laura's arms sounded like a heavenly change from her father's hell-fire and brimstone threats which he preached to the natives as he browbeat them into accepting his beliefs as the only true and real way to eternal salvation.

"Where will the christening take place?" Rose asked, hoping she wouldn't be told it was in the river. That scenario would be a little too close to her past experiences.

Laura smiled, not just at her, but at all the women. "I know Brody thinks it's silly of me, but I want to have Charlotte christened in Yuma, in the same church where I was christened. Reverend Wesley is still there, and he's the one who christened me when I was her age." She smoothed at the peach fuzz on her daughter's crown. "I know it's farther for everyone to travel, but it's important to me. I also hope, something so happy at that church will erase the last of Brody's bad memories from something that happened there a long time ago."

Privately, Rose wondered what bad memories Brody might have from a church. She contented herself with saying, "I'm sure no one will mind."

"And you still want to come back here to the café after?" Georgina asked anxiously.

Rose shot her employer a surprised look. To her, it was clear the ladies considered Georgina one of them. Yet today it became equally clear that, as much as she might like to be one of them, Georgina didn't feel the same sense of belonging as the women did who were married to the Mason brothers.

But what did she know about the way normal families operated?

"Of course," Laura said. "Bullet is home. The café is a large part of that."

"Hawkes was across the street earlier." Bishop sidled up to Brody, the eldest of the group and the unofficial head of the family.

Brody, whose attention had been focused on his wife and her friends, tensed, hands fisted. "When?"

"Rose spotted him earlier. Didn't mention it till later, though, just as we all came back inside."

"Did you look around outside? Everything all right?"

Bishop nodded. "Didn't see anything out of place. You really think he'd try something with this many folks around?"

They both fell silent, knowing there was no safety in numbers. Hawkes had effectively disrupted more than one of the weddings lately.

"I wouldn't put anything past him."

Brody must have noticed the furtive way Bishop was watching Rose as they spoke. "Do I detect a little gleam in her eye when the new gal looks in your direction?"

Bishop snorted. "More like she's tapping me to do her a favor."

"Maybe she caught your road show when you and Barron were fleecing unsuspecting folks from their hard-earned wages," Brody said.

"Folks shouldn't gamble if they can't afford to lose," Bishop said. "You're no different. None of us are, when it comes right down to it."

"Being lucky with a deck of cards is a far cry from throwing a fight," Brody said.

Bishop pressed his lips together. He wasn't proud of certain things he'd done in the past, but it had been a matter of survival. Them or him and Barron. And he still felt that way. Maybe that's why Rose was managing to push all the right buttons.

"Just watch yourself," Brody said. "A woman in need can be a formidable opponent. And an even more formidable enemy."

"Amen to that."

As afternoon stretched into early evening, the wedding celebration began to die down. Parents rounded up over-tired children to take them home. Rose made herself useful helping some of the other town ladies including Georgina clear up the hall, all the while keeping one eye on Bishop. She was determined to enlist his help, no matter what it took. If he left today, she might not get another chance. She'd be stuck in town, and he'd be out on the ranch where he lived with the others.

"Storm is getting ready to toss her bouquet," Georgina said. "You'd best get up there with the other young, single gals."

"Why?" Rose asked.

"It's rumored good luck smiles on whoever catches the bouquet."

Rose could use some good luck in her quest to find Lily. "What about you? Why aren't you going up?"

Georgina flushed. "Oh, I couldn't. I leave that to the younger ones."

"You're hardly in your dotage," Rose said. "Besides, couldn't we all use some good luck?"

Over Georgina's half-hearted protest, Rose took the other woman's arm and herded her up to the front of the room just in time to witness the ceremonial removal of the bride's blue garter. Storm stood on a chair while Blake made a big production out of reaching under her dress, one hand over his eyes as he pretended not to peek at his new wife's partly exposed leg.

"What's he doing?" Rose asked curiously. This was her first time seeing white folks get married.

"It's traditional," Georgina said. "It's long been believed that having a piece of something the bride wore would bring good luck. Except folks sometimes got carried away and started ripping at the bride's gown. That's when this new tradition was started, where the groom removes the bride's garter and tosses it out to the bachelors. The idea being, the one who catches it will be the next one to find himself married."

Rose saw the way Storm colored prettily as she hung on to the shoulder of her new husband for balance. The men were clapping and making off-color jokes about Blake fumbling his way through the wedding night ritual.

Reluctantly, it seemed, the twins and one of the other Masons shuffled up behind the other more eager town bachelors, amid much ribbing from their married brothers as to who would be next. The garter arced over everyone's heads through the air and toward Bishop, who made no effort to reach for it.

The item fell at his feet, which earned a chorus of "boos" from the wedding guests. Bishop flushed all shades of red as he picked up the garter and stuffed it in his pocket.

"A true Mason," Georgina said. "They all act like they aren't the least bit interested. Till one day love hits them over the head with a sledge-hammer."

Rose bit back her comment that it would take more than a sledge- hammer to get her interested in a man in that way.

Up ahead, still standing on the chair, Storm turned her back to the crowd and gave her bouquet a toss. Following its progress with her eyes, Rose stepped aside to give Georgina an equal chance for the supposed good luck, but at the last minute, the floral nosegay seemed to spin right into her arms.

Triumphantly Rose raised it overhead, to a round of cheers and clapping and whistling. She lowered her face to the nosegay and breathed in deeply. The flowers' sweet fragrance was more glorious than anything she recalled ever smelling.

She smiled broadly at those nearby. "Bring on the good luck," she said, not understanding the laughter from those listening. She watched Barron elbow his twin and point her way.

Bolstered by the bouquet in her hand, and with far more bravado than she was feeling, Rose crossed the room to the twins. "How about I make you a deal? You help me with my mission, finding my sister, and I'll help you with yours."

Bishop's mouth tightened in disapproval. "We don't need your help."

"You think that now. I happen to know better."

Barron scoffed. "You have no clue what we're about."

"Working at the café, a girl overhears a lot. I know what Hawkes is up to. I know who is for and against him. And I know exactly how you can strip him of his power."

CHAPTER 3

"What do you know about Hawkes?" Bishop asked. He'd bet his last dollar she was lying. Didn't women all have a habit of saying whatever a gent wanted to hear in order to get their way?

"I know Don Lucas and the other investors are fed up with Hawkes and his empty promises. They're working on a plan to call in their loans. He'll be scrambling for new financing."

"How does this help us?" Barron asked.

"What if there happened to be the arrival in town of a wealthy benefactress? One who appears totally smitten with Hawkes and willing to go along with whatever he suggests —, all the while working with you both to destroy him."

"It'll never happen," Bishop said dismissively.

"Trust me, I know exactly how to make it work."

"How? You play the benefactress?" Barron said.

Rose shook her head. "He's seen me around the cafe. We have to find my sister. She can help make this work."

Bishop opened his mouth to tell her to go peddle her

hare-brained scheme elsewhere, only to be interrupted by Barron's none-too-gentle grip on his arm.

"We don't do anything without talking to Brody and the others," Barron said. "Give us a few days to consult with them."

"Don't take too long," Rose said. "The offer is time-sensitive." She turned and walked away.

Bishop stared at his twin. "You can't be serious!"

"Of course not," Barron said. "But she did get me started thinking. It's possible we've been coming at this all wrong."

ROSE RELEASED her pent-up breath as she walked across the room to where Georgina and some of the other ladies were doing the last of the tidying up. She looked down to see that her hand holding the bouquet was shaking.

What had come over her? Pretending to the twins that she knew far more than she did. Sure, she'd heard the odd comment here and there in the café, but for the most part she was as much in the dark as everyone else.

And, assuming they managed to find Lily, then what? There was no way Lily could take on the role Rose had just proposed, a wealthy socialite interested in working with Hawkes. Lily knew even less about the world than Rose did. She certainly had no experience with men, let alone how to handle and manipulate someone as evil as Hawkes was rumored to be.

"I knew that bouquet was meant for you," Georgina said with a big grin. "And Bishop with the garter. What was he talking to you about just now?"

Rose looked down, pleased to see that her hand had stopped shaking as Georgina watched her, eager for news.

The other woman had been so kind, Rose felt guilty lying to her. Hadn't she had it beaten into her from infancy that telling falsehoods was the root of all evil?

"He was asking me about a few of the restaurant patrons. No one I knew. I think maybe he was on the lookout for someone traveling through."

"No one travels through Bullet," Georgina said, suspicion darkening her gaze. "It's the end of the road. Few years ago, some of the townsfolk hoped the railway would come through here and really wake up the place. Make it more prosperous. But the railway gents took one look around and high-tailed it back to Yuma. Bullet will never be anything more than this same dusty little village, known as a place where a lot of killing went on back in the day."

Deftly Rose changed the subject. "What can I give you a hand with?"

Georgina handed her a wooden crate full of clean glassware. "Do you mind taking this over to the café for me?"

"Not at all."

Dusk was falling upon the town as she walked the short distance from the hall to the café. A slight breeze rustled a lone piece of paper as it blew across the deserted, dusty road in front of her.

The café lay in darkness, but she knew where Georgina kept the key, so she set down her burden and unlocked the door. All was dark and still inside and she debated lighting a lamp, but it seemed silly when she would just be going right back out again.

Her flowers rested atop the clean glassware, their fragrance wafting her way. She needed to put them in water to make them last. She carried the nosegay through the dark into the kitchen, laid the flowers on the sideboard, and carefully felt her way along the shelf over the sink until she found an empty mason jar. She placed it in the sink and pumped enough water to fill it halfway.

She placed the flowers in the water and fluffed them up, rewarded by another rush of fragrance from their petals. Her first nosegay of flowers. Her life had come a long way in a short time. All she needed was Lily here to share it with.

Rose was certain, once she found her sister, she'd be able to convince her there was no reason to return to their parents and that cold, empty life as daughters of a missionary. They were more than old enough to be on their own.

She whirled when the outside door closed with a bang. "Who's there? Georgina? Anyone?" Her heart was thudding so hard in her chest, she was certain the sound would be audible to anyone who was there, alerting them to her presence. She caught and held her breath, strained her ears, but didn't hear a thing.

She had just started to inch her way from the kitchen to the front of the café when she heard voices and laughter outside. The door opened and she could make out Georgina and some of the other women, all carrying bins.

"Heavens, Rose. What are you doing here in the dark? Light a lantern."

"I..." Her lips were dry. Her voice sounded unnaturally loud. "I planned to come right back. I just stopped to put the flowers in water."

The lantern flared to life, and Rose's gaze searched the dark corners of the empty room. Had she just imagined that someone had been there with her? As the others trooped into the kitchen with their loads, she moved to pick up the bin of glassware she'd left on a table out front. Lying on top of the glasses was a folded piece of paper. She snatched it up and shoved it in her bosom before anyone saw.

It was hours later when things at the café were more or

less put to rights and she was in her room for the night that she had a chance to take out the note and read it.

Go away. Or yer sister gets hurt!

～

A FEW DAYS after the wedding, Bishop and Barron hunted Brody down near the irrigation ditch he was digging. No one else was around. "Got a minute?" Barron asked.

Brody put down his shovel and swiped his forearm across his face as he tipped his hat back.

"Why do I get the feeling, when you two make a point to get me alone, you've got a thing or two up your sleeve?"

Bishop exchanged a glance with his brother.

Barron nodded and picked up the conversation. "Just been thinking about Hawkes. How we can maybe get things resolved once and for all."

"Pretty sure we're all tired of looking over our shoulders," Bishop chimed in. "Heard a rumor he might be in financial trouble. That his partners want out."

Brody nodded and picked up his shovel. "That much is true."

"So," Bishop said. "What if we were to set up one last con? Sucker-punch him in the wallet, enough to make him lose face around here. We can even make his death look like suicide."

Brody's face darkened. "Been giving this quite a bit of thought, have you?"

"That's right." Barron nodded.

"And you'd like to be the ones who kill him. An eye for an eye and all that."

"He killed our brother," Bishop said.

"So you figure that gives you first crack to end Hawkes's worthless, miserable life?"

Bishop licked his lips. Somehow this wasn't going the way he had anticipated. "If not us, then who?"

Brody appeared to ponder the question. "Bradley for starters. Since it seems the man raped his mother."

"But—"

"And then there was that young girl Hawkes killed and got off scot-free. Braydon's sister by all accounts."

Bishop looked over at his brother. Brody brought up incidents they hadn't taken into consideration.

"Ever wonder why Hawkes was on my radar long before your brother Joe got between him and that knife?"

"I thought it had something to do with Hawkes and your uncle," Barron said.

"More than that," Brody said. "Hawkes gunned my old man down right in front of me. Made good and sure I knew he enjoyed every second of it."

"We didn't know," Bishop said.

"Did Hawkes see you there?" Barron asked.

"Oh, he saw me all right. Looked me in the eye seconds after he pulled the trigger." Brody sucked in a breath as if the memory made it difficult to breathe. "We made a pact that night Joe died, the seven of us. No one goes it alone on a one-man vendetta. Pretty sure you'll find out that Blake and Ben have their own reasons for wanting a part of seeing Hawkes dead as well." Brody turned back and picked up his shovel. "Anything else?"

Bishop shook his head, aware that Barron mirrored the move.

"Then I suggest you both get back to work."

~

ROSE MADE a grab for the soapy plate as it slipped from her hand, caught it and hugged it against her, mindless of the wet spot it left on the front of her apron. It wasn't fair to take out her frustration on the innocent dishes at Georgina's café. Besides which, she couldn't afford to have her pay docked for broken crockery.

"You all right, Rose?" Georgina gave her a questioning look, and not for the first time.

She nodded. Nothing much missed Georgina's eagle eye. And Rose knew she had been a bit agitated since the day of the wedding and her discussion with the Mason twins. Topped off by that note. No one in town other than the twins knew about Lily. Did they? Unless the kidnapper was there in town.

How she yearned for a world where she didn't need a man's help. Truth was, she *did* need men's help. Her attempt to travel around disguised as a boy had been a dismal failure. And as a young woman traveling alone in the territory, she left herself far too vulnerable to be of use to Lily if she ever did manage to find her.

She greatly admired the women she had met since coming here to Bullet. Henrietta had traveled vastly abroad and clearly thought nothing of striking out on her own. Storm, too, had traveled the countryside on her own in the book-lending wagon.

Both of those ladies came from upbringings vastly different from hers. Storm had been a mail-order bride, and then a widow. Henrietta, with her Argentinian background, had achieved independence thanks to an inheritance from her English grandmother.

In the world Rose came from, a woman had little or no value, other than to do the bidding of the males in her life—

in her case, her cold, controlling father. Daughters were treated like a commodity, a liability, or both.

It hadn't taken Rose long to learn how truly vulnerable a woman alone could be. She remembered when she first met the twins. She'd been trying to pick Bishop's pocket. She thought she'd got away with it too, until they turned the tables and trapped her at a game they played far better than she did.

Her retaliation, attempting to steal the book wagon, hadn't gone over well, and clearly they were more than weary of her antics by the time they found her stowed away. Luckily, by the time she was discovered, the three of them were already in Bullet.

She was grateful they elected to deliver her to Georgina. The good woman took her in and put her to work. No one here judged her, not even those who knew the true story of their meeting.

She needed to find her sister, and fast, something she couldn't manage without the help of the twins. She wished it was otherwise. She also wasn't convinced they bought her story that she had a plan to bring down Hawkes. Which meant she had better come up with one soon, just in case.

"It sure is nice to have an extra pair of hands," Georgina said.

"I appreciate you taking me in and giving me the chance," Rose said. Life on the street, her only other option, would greatly hinder her goal. She might never find out where that low life had taken Lily.

"Ma was doing her best," Georgina said. "But it was really getting to be too much for her. We'll close down early Saturday," she added. "Give ourselves time to get prettied up and drive to Yuma for the christening."

Laura had lent Rose a gown to wear to the wedding,

something she claimed no longer fit her since she'd had baby Charlotte. Rose had accepted it gratefully. She wondered if she might borrow it again for the christening.

∼

HAWKES FACED off against Reverend Wesley in the sacristy, pleased to see the other man's hands shake as he splashed a good measure of communion wine into the chalice and downed it in a single gulp.

"What you're asking is not possible."

"I say it is," Hawkes said, his voice deceptively smooth. No point spooking the reverend, when the man had his uses. "A family emergency took you out of town unexpectedly. Luckily the deacon just happens to be here to fill in for you at the christening. And what an honor that will be."

He slid paper and pen across the desk to the reverend, who plopped into his chair as if his legs would no longer support him.

"Now write the note. Unless you want your wife to learn all about your dirty little secrets. And what you like to do with those pretty little Mexican *chiquitas*."

Wesley's hand continued to shake so badly, he could barely put pen to paper.

Once he was done, Hawkes looked over the note and nodded. As soon as the ink dried, he took it and folded it into neat thirds.

He dropped a pile of bills onto the desk. "Now take your wife on a little train ride out of town for a few days. Maybe you can get her interested in the same games as your little girls." He pasted on a smile. "And don't worry. I'll see to it that Mason gets this note in plenty of time."

"But ... My congregation."

"Saints and sinners." Hawkes smirked. "They'll all get by without you for a few days."

~

THE DAY of the christening dawned warm and sunny like any other. As soon as they were done serving breakfast, Georgina closed down the café, and she and Rose rushed to get changed.

Seated next to Georgina in her rickety buggy, Rose smoothed the fabric of the gown that Laura had generously insisted she keep. She had never owned something this pretty before. After weeks of dressing like a boy, it was nice to wear something feminine for a change. And something that didn't have an apron overtop.

They pulled up in front of the church in Yuma, just behind the Masons' entourage. Brody and Laura and baby Charlotte were in the first conveyance along with Braydon and Henrietta, the godparents. A second rig was behind them with the other two recently married couples.

Rose was quick to spot Bishop, circling around the group on horseback along with his twin and one of the other men. "Which brother is that with the twins?"

Georgina flushed prettily. "That's Benjamin."

"He's very handsome," Rose said.

Benjamin sat tall in the saddle, holding his rifle in such a way one might think it had been born in his hand. Rose noticed the way all the men cast vigilant eyes up and down the street, which was bustling with activity on this busy Saturday afternoon.

Georgina stared down at the reins in her hand. "Really? I hadn't noticed. No time for things like that."

Rose laughed. "I was raised out in the wilds, spent half

34

my time with the native people, and I can still appreciate a good-looking man when I see one. All the Mason men are very handsome," she added. "Don't you think?"

"I suppose." Georgina was suddenly beet-red in the face. "We'd best get inside. Here, you'll need this." She passed Rose a headscarf.

"What's this for?"

"It's considered respectful for a woman to cover her head in the house of the Lord."

Rose noticed the other women were either wearing hats or also covering their hair so quickly followed suit. As the daughter of a missionary, she had been brought up believing the entire good green earth was the house of the Almighty. Head-covering had never been part of the worship.

Inside the church, sunlight filtered through stained-glass windows and cast multi-colored light upon the wooden pews. The air was faintly tinged with the smell of burning candle wax. Rose had spent very little time in churches. Most of her father's sermons had taken place in the great outdoors, what he liked to call "God's chapel". Christenings were done in the river.

She followed Georgina into a pew a respectful distance behind where the family members all took seats at the front. Today promised to be a new and interesting experience.

Once again, she was aware of the camaraderie and caring among the Mason family as Brody made sure Laura was comfortably settled in the front pew, Charlotte sleeping peacefully in her mother's arms. The christening font stood off to one side, covered with a large, dome-shaped metal lid.

One by one the rest of the family, with the exception of Amanda, drifted in and took their seats at the front. Unlike the women, the men had all removed their hats. Rose guessed every religion had its rules. Her father had always touted a christening as a way of wiping the person's soul clean of sin. Looking at little Charlotte, it was hard to believe the baby's soul needed purifying.

Softly at first, the faint swirling notes of a hymn could be heard wafting through the small church from the choir loft. Rose craned her head to the back of the church and upward to where Amanda sat at the piano. Rose didn't know the hymn— church music had not been a part of her upbringing— but it sounded both soothing and happy. A perfect choice for this occasion.

She stared at the back of Bishop's head, noticing the way his dark hair curled against his collar. His broad shoulders strained at the seams of his chambray shirt. She wondered if he and his brother had been christened at birth. As if he felt her eyes on him, he turned and caught her gaze.

Drat! He'd caught her staring.

His mouth quirked in an acknowledging smile, and butterflies chased around her insides. She'd seen him smile before, usually with a mocking pull to his lips as if he didn't really mean it. This smile was different. It felt intimate somehow, as if it was intended solely for her and her alone. Nothing to do with those nearby.

The church's cavernous interior echoed as people shuffled their feet and cleared their throats. She heard the occasional whisper from up front. Where was the clergyman?

No sooner did the thought surface than she heard the click of a door opening on the far side of the altar. A man wearing religious vestments appeared.

The music trailed to a stop as the parents and godparents rose and approached the christening font. The clergyman removed the lid and opened his bible. As the ceremony started Rose found her attention wandering. How far away could Lily be? How soon before Rose could find her? Who left that note telling her to go away? Lily's captor? If that was the case, her sister could be closer by than she might have guessed.

Abruptly her thoughts were interrupted by a faint scream. She looked up to see the clergyman had hold of baby Charlotte and was dipping her headfirst into the water, holding her there. Everyone jumped to their feet, weapons drawn, as Braydon and Brody both tackled the minister.

The altercation was short-lived. After a few scary moments of a skirmish among the men, Brody had his daughter safely in his arms. And Braydon had the clergyman in a chokehold.

Suddenly the air was split by maniacal laughter coming from the back of the building. Heads craned to the choir loft, where Hawkes stood, larger than life, Amanda in front of him like a shield, with a gun pointed at her head.

CHAPTER 4

Bishop heard a low growl from Bradley, next to him. Something guttural and not quite human.

"Easy." Bishop spoke from the side of his mouth, one arm tensed and ready to restrain the other man from doing something rash. He could only imagine how Bradley must feel, seeing that scumbag with his hands on his wife, holding a gun at her head.

"Now that I have your attention!" Hawkes laughed again, a mad cackle that echoed from the rafters of the church. "Nice of you to all gather together under one roof. Makes my plan easy."

"Let her go, Hawkes," Brody said.

"A man holding a baby!" Hawkes sneered. "Not in much of a position to be calling any shots are you?"

He raised his other hand to reveal a second gun, which he pointed Brody's way. "Kind of a small target, but I bet I could kill the brat with one, well-placed shot. With any luck the bullet would rip right through it and kill you at the same time."

"What do you want?" Brody said.

Hawkes took his time answering. "For one, I'd be much obliged if you would unhand my man down there. He plays a pretty credible holy man, wouldn't you agree?"

Bishop shifted his gaze from the front of the church where Braydon reluctantly unhanded the fake clergyman, back to the loft.

Amanda had lost all color. Even at this distance, he could see her freckles standing out against the translucent white of her skin.

"Sorry for busting in on your gathering," Hawkes said. "Have to say I was rather hurt not to be asked to be godfather." He laughed as if he had just made the biggest joke ever.

"I asked you what you want," Brody said through gritted teeth.

"You know the answer to that. I plan to take over your ranch. But more than that, I intend to enjoy the process of wrestling it away from you. Seeing you reduced to your position of loser, same as when you first showed up. Unwanted trash. Good for nothing. Unable to protect your family. Like today. Useless scum."

With a shove that sent Amanda reeling toward the edge of the railing, Hawkes was gone.

Bishop moved first, Bradley on his heels, as they darted toward the spiral staircase at the rear of the church. He knew the other men had scattered in various directions in order to throw out a net to catch Hawkes.

He took the steps two at a time and burst into the loft, where Amanda sat limply behind the piano. Wordlessly, she pointed to a second staircase, one that led directly outside.

Bishop left Bradley to comfort his wife while he raced

outside where the others prowled around, guns drawn. Brody shook his head. "He's gone. Cleared out of here like a vanishing act."

Braydon came around the side of the church. "The other man's gone as well."

Bishop and the others all looked to Brody as the remainder of the family and friends cautiously made their way from the church to gather nearby. He caught the occasional low murmur from the group, who were all clearly shaken up by what had just happened.

"Hawkes is getting desperate," Brody said. "He never used to show his hand, just hit from the shadows."

Brody approached Laura and laid a protective arm around her shoulders as she hugged their daughter close and made comforting, cooing noises to the baby. Charlotte was wide awake, her dark peach fuzz hair already starting to dry from the dousing. Her bonnet had been lost in the commotion.

Brody glanced over at Georgina. "You still want us all over at the café for the after-party?"

Georgina squared her shoulders. "What else would I do with all that food we prepared?"

"Hawkes doesn't take kindly to those who take our side against him."

"That would be pretty much the entire town, now wouldn't it?" Georgina said with a sniff. "I may just ban him from the café after that little stunt in the church. I don't need customers like him."

Bishop noticed Amanda had regained some of her color. Bradley held her as if he would never let her out of his sight. Bishop pondered Hawkes's tactics. Was the man just proving one more time what an easy target they could be?

As the others mounted up or climbed into buggies, Barron came up to him. "You know what we have to do, don't you?"

Bishop nodded as he returned his gun to its holster. "Looks like we need to go find ourselves a missing girl."

The trip to Bullet was uneventful, although Bishop, like everyone else rode stiffly, on his guard, eyes peeled. As they reached town, he took the time to notice how good the café looked, given the expansion and improvements Georgina had made in the past year.

Inside, Bishop hung back as the others found seats and Georgina and Rose busied themselves putting out a selection of sandwiches and sweets for the guests from the christening. He couldn't quite relax, even though he knew no one except invited guests would make it through the door.

Barron sidled up to him. "Ever wish we hadn't made that promise to Brody?"

As usual, Barron was reading his mind. "You mean not to deal with Hawkes on our own? Without the blessing of the others?"

At the time, fresh on the heels of witnessing Hawkes kill their brother, the twins had welcomed the solidarity of the Mason brotherhood, aware every one of the others had reasons for wanting to see Hawkes get his.

Yet years later, despite his continued reign of terror, one arrest, and several attacks and unexplained murders, Hawkes was still a free man.

"Exactly. How much more will Hawkes get away with before his time comes?"

Bishop wondered the same thing. He looked over to where Rose bustled about filling coffee cups and water glasses. Could she be trusted?

"Think we can trust her?" Barron asked.

Bishop clapped him on the shoulder. "Get out of my head! At this point, I don't think we have a choice. Rose wants something powerful bad and so do we. Banded together, the three of us could prove unstoppable."

"I understand what she said about family," Barron said. "Nothing would stand in my way if you went missing."

Bishop nodded. "Same for me. I'd do anything. It's clear Rose has that same dogged determination."

Barron nodded. "I'll leave it to you to give her the good news. I'll go let Brody know we'll be gone for a while."

Bishop grinned. "What are you going to tell him? That we have a book-lending emergency?"

"Given what we've done in the past, the cons we've pulled, I should be able to come up with something plausible."

ROSE BUSIED herself putting out a tray of pickles. Her hands were still a little unsteady from the incident earlier at the church, and the pickled onions rolled around, ruining Georgina's fancy display. Every time Rose thought about that evil man holding a gun to Amanda, her thoughts migrated to Lily, and the very real possibility her sister was in the hands of someone far worse.

She'd seen evil in her day and plenty of it. Men slaughtering others for the sheer sport of the kill. But they always traveled in a pack, like rabid wolves. Seeing one man threaten an innocent family with such arrogant nonchalance, witnessing his smug, self-assured superiority, made her want to kill him herself.

How she regretted that stupid suggestion she had made to the twins earlier. Clearly they found her as dumb and naïve as her entire act. To pretend she and her sister could pull off a scheme to bring Hawkes down in a way the Masons couldn't.

She smashed her balled-up fists together in agitation.

"Whoa!"

Before she could move, she found her hands caught and held in Bishop's much larger, much stronger hands. Which only made her angry. He always caught her at her worst. Saw her vulnerable. Alone.

"You fixing to punch somebody out?"

"Maybe." She wrenched her hands free, aware she only managed it because he loosened his grip.

"The man who took your sister?" Bishop asked.

"For starters," Rose said haughtily, rubbing her wrists. She could still feel the unforgiving steel of his grip. "Followed by you and your brother because you won't help me find her."

He stared down at her, a serious look on his handsome face. Why had she never noticed before just how blue his eyes were? She'd not seen the ocean, but his eyes were the color she imagined when she thought of a storm-tossed sea, and fringed by the darkest lashes she had ever seen. Her own and Lily's eyelashes were much lighter in shade.

"Barron and I were just talking about that very thing," Bishop said.

"What very thing?" she said defiantly. "Your smart decision not to help the dumb girl?"

"You're neither dumb nor a girl," Bishop said, his eyes moving over her in a way that made her aware of her feminine assets, and the way they were displayed in her newly-acquired gown. "Don't recall that dress ever looking quite so good on Laura. Not that she's not an attractive lady," he added quickly. "But she's always been Brody's lady. That color suits you better than it did her."

Rose felt heat creep into her cheeks and glanced down to where the toe of her worn boot peeped from beneath her hemline. Was he pitying her in her hand-me-downs? Softening his words by adding something nice?

Never having been on the receiving end of a compliment, even a double-edged one, she was unsure of the expected reaction. Did one say "thank you"? Or just nod in a gracious way, as if fielding a compliment from an attractive man was nothing new?

Bishop cleared his throat as if he, too, found the air between them suddenly thick. "What Barron and I were discussing was how we would feel if one of us suddenly got grabbed up. Sure as shooting we'd move heaven and earth to get the other one found. Nothing would stop us."

"Nice for you," she said, with a faint trace of bitterness. "Things are different out there when you're a woman, especially a woman on her own."

Bishop nodded. "Had us an idea. For helping find your sister, I mean."

Rose straightened. Had she heard Bishop right? "You changed your mind about helping me?"

"We never outright said no," Bishop said patiently. "We just weren't about to go chasing off without some sort of a plan in place. Seems that's mostly what you've spent your time doing so far, and it hasn't exactly panned out."

Rose nodded. She did tend to act first and think later, but she wasn't about to admit that to Bishop.

"Barron and me being twins gives us a bit of an advantage."

"How so?"

"Figure we'll pull into the towns same as we always do, and set up the book-lending. Except this time, I'll introduce you as my new wife. Act like it's just the two of us taking the wagon out. That way, Barron and I can cover twice as much ground and no one will know. Whichever one of us they see, they'll think it's me."

She narrowed her gaze suspiciously. "Why do you need to introduce me as your wife?"

Bishop blew out a breath. "'Cause I don't have a sister. And if you think I have designs on you, you can just turn that thought right out of your head. Folks around here are old-fashioned. A man and a woman traveling around in any sort of wagon overnight, who aren't married to each other, that just wouldn't be seemly. We also won't outright be asking about Lily. Just inquiring about any newcomers in the area. Let folks think we're just trying to drum up more business."

Rose hated to admit it, but the twins had put far more thought into the logistics of the quest to find Lily than she had. She tended to just rush into things without any fore-thought, blunder her way through and wonder why nothing worked out.

Too impulsive by half, she'd been told all through her growing-up years.

Why aren't you more like Lily? had been a refrain she'd heard so often, she closed her ears to it.

"As long as you both realize I'm not sitting back at the wagon all meek and useless while you save the day."

Bishop's eyes twinkled. "Don't much see you being all meek and useless in any situation. But you told us you thought the man might have sold her. Means we need to check out the..." He paused for a beat. "Fancy ladies' houses. Not the kind of place for you to be in."

She jutted out her chin. One more time, men taking charge and her expected to do as she was told. "So what do you see me doing to help?"

Bishop opened his mouth as if to say something, then thought better of it. "Be best if you tried to make friends with some of the ladies in the towns we visit. They'll know if any of the ranchers or farmers in the area has recently acquired a new bride."

"You think she might have been sold in marriage?" Rose felt faint at the thought.

"Only two things I see a lady getting sold for. Wifely duties or whoring. We'll see to one while you look into the other. Church ladies would be a good place for you to start."

"What should I tell Georgina? I mean, seeing as I won't be around to help out for a while." She played back her own words. Had she just said that? Made it sound like she'd be coming back here? Not that she had anyplace else to go.

"Tell Georgina there's a family emergency. That much is true. Ask her to drive you to Yuma and let you off at the train station. Best if folks here in town don't know you're going with us."

She nodded and swallowed. Part of her wanted to thank him, but thanks were premature. After they found Lily would be the proper time to express her gratitude.

BISHOP REINED to a stop once he reached his intended vantage point near Hawkes's place and pulled the spyglass out of his pocket. It had taken a while for him and Barron to search out the ideal watching spot to monitor comings and goings around Hawkes's ranch. They both knew Brody would be livid if he knew what they were up to.

Brody insisted he had a plan to take down Hawkes when the time was right. In Bishop's mind the right time was now. That stunt Hawkes pulled in the church wasn't something he was about to sit still for. He'd been unable to stop Hawkes from killing his brother Joe. He'd be damned if Hawkes got close enough ever again to hurt someone he cared about.

From behind, he heard the furtive sounds of a horse approaching and wheeled about, gun drawn.

"You know I could drop you before you had a bead on me."

Bishop relaxed when he recognized Ben's voice. "Anyone ever teach you not to sneak up on a body?" he asked as Ben reached his side.

"What's that?" Ben indicated the spyglass.

"Souvenir from the old days," Bishop said. He handed it over for Ben to try out. "Barron and I took it off this mark, who claimed he got it from a pirate. Brings things far away up close."

"You don't say." Ben let out a low whistle when he looked through the device. He handed it back carefully. "How come none of us know you have this?"

Bishop shrugged. "I dunno. Forgot about it for a long time. Recently, Barron and I figured it would come in useful out here. Keep a closer eye on that vermin."

"Brody told me you boys are hitting the road for a few. Thought I'd see if you needed a third."

"You suddenly interested in the book lending?"

"Nope," Ben said, his clear gaze leveled on Bishop. "And I got a hunch neither are you."

Bishop blew out a breath. "And Brody?"

"Brody tends to believe folks till they give him good reason not to."

"Barron and I got ourselves something of a delicate nature going on this trip. Afraid another body along for the ride would call the wrong kind of attention to what we're about."

"Promise you'll be careful?" Ben said. "And don't even try taking on Hawkes without the rest of us."

Bishop murmured something unintelligible. "Tell you what," he said. "How about you take over here whenever you get the chance? You can fill us in when we get back." He passed over the spyglass as he spoke. "You'll be needing this."

Benjamin stared down at the spyglass Bishop slapped into his hand. "I mean what I said. No cavalry, you and your brother. We're in this together. We all have our reasons for wanting our go at Hawkes."

"What's yours?" Bishop asked.

Ben raised the spyglass to his eye. His lips thinned as he stared at Hawkes's ranch. "It's personal."

To Rose's surprise, Georgina readily agreed to drive her to Yuma for the train. Once there, she managed to find a spot to stop the buggy near the station before she turned to Rose. "You promise you're coming back?"

"I promise." Rose jumped out quickly before Georgina could plead one more time with her not to leave. She knew the other woman meant well and felt bad about having to fib. She looked up and tried for a reassuring half- smile. "This is just something I have to do. Thank you for under- standing."

Georgina gave her head a shake. "I don't understand at all. But then I never had a sister, either."

"I'll be back before you even notice I'm gone." Rose gave the horse a slap on its rump. She'd already caught sight of the book wagon around the next corner and wanted Georgina well on her way before she noticed it, as well.

She blew out a breath as she watched Georgina turn the buggy around and head back toward Bullet. Only then did she dart across the street to where the twins waited. She knew it was Barron holding the reins, even though the two of them were dressed in identical checkered shirts and leather vests.

Bishop climbed out, grabbed her small sack with a change of clothing, and helped her in. Her heart beat crazy with excitement as she shifted along, sandwiched between the two men on the narrow driving bench.

"Where are we going first?" she asked.

"Castle Dome Landing," Bishop said. "Their post office closed down a few years back, so we picked up some mail from here for a few of the residents. Should give us a good excuse to nose around."

"Not only that," Barron said. "It's an easy steam ship ride from there back to Yuma and other parts."

Rose's eyes widened. "If Lily and her captor were traveling by steam ship, someone had to have seen them. You think she could be here in Yuma?"

"No reason to think so," Barron said. "But if they're still in the territory, we should be able to find out which way they were headed."

Excitement fizzled. Rose slumped. "They could be anyplace. Mexico. California. Anywhere."

She didn't miss the look the twins exchanged. She straightened. "What? What are you not telling me?"

"It's not like that," Bishop said. "We don't know anything more than you."

"Way we see it," Barron said, "traveling with an unwilling prisoner is kind of a liability in these parts. Easy to draw unwanted attention. We're of a mind he'd be looking to unload her as soon as possible."

"Either that or he plans to keep her," Bishop said. "Someplace no one will ever find her."

Rose's heart began beating fast again, but from anxiety this time. "What are we waiting for?"

They stopped a short distance outside of town so Barron could hand Bishop the reins and climb into the back of the wagon.

"It doesn't look very busy here." Rose bit back her disappointment when they reached the center of town.

Bishop shot her a look. "Why do you think they closed the post office? It was booming here when the mine was going. Busy as Yuma."

"And now?"

"Now folks are waiting and hoping for the mine to reopen."

"Boom and bust," Rose said. Her father had often preached the evils of chasing wealth. How riches destroyed a man's heart and soul.

"We'll stop in at the store first," Bishop said.

After they stopped, he climbed down from the wagon and glanced around with a bemused smile. "Kind of sad to see it like this. Not that long since Barron and I had ourselves quite the time here. Mining money was plentiful, and it was easy to work our cons."

"You sound almost proud of that. Taking advantage of others."

Bishop slanted her a glance. She saw the way he got defensive and knew she had hit a nerve.

"Never took anything from folks who couldn't afford it," he muttered.

"How do you know?"

"Folks shouldn't gamble if they can't afford to lose."

"What if it was a father gambling away the family food money?"

"Then he doesn't deserve his family." Bishop's look darkened, as if he was lost in memories.

"Yet his family has no choice."

Bishop straightened his shoulders. "Indians killed our parents when we were young. Joe was older. He hid Barron and I. After it was over—" he swallowed thickly— "Joe took us to live with an aunt and uncle while he set off looking for work. He heard there was mining out this way. Not sure how he wound up working for Hawkes. All I know is Aunt hated having "two more mouths to feed." Barron and I took off to look for Joe as soon as we were old enough. It's true we conned folks along the way. And true, too, Barron took out some of his anger through fighting. But he never killed anybody."

Bishop was silent so long, Rose wondered if that was the end of the story.

"And now Barron's keeping all that anger bottled up inside. And you make sure he doesn't explode."

He acted as if he didn't hear her.

"Joe knew Brody had room for us on the ranch." He sighed. "Wish he would have stayed there with us, but Hawkes strung him along with promises of big money."

"Why did Hawkes kill your brother?"

His mouth tightened as he picked up the reins. "That we don't know. What we do know is that he enjoyed it. Makes him less than human in my eyes. Which is why killing is too good for him."

She cocked her head. "How come you're not angry the same way Barron is?"

"How do you know I'm not?"

"Same reason I knew you would be the one to help me find my sister."

CHAPTER 5

Bishop shot a sideways look at his companion as he started up the wagon. What had come over him? Telling her all that stuff. He didn't need to justify one single thing in his life, especially to this gal, who acted like she thought she knew everything about him. She had no idea.

Who cared if she thought he was a good guy or not? Wasn't it enough that he and Barron were helping her find her sister?

After that, who knew? Maybe she could be some help with Hawkes. And he wouldn't waste time feeling guilty if helping them landed her in danger.

Or would he?

In no time, they arrived at the store. He reached behind him and banged on the wall of the wagon so Barron would know they were here, then turned to Rose.

"Think you can pretend to like me? At least enough so folks believe we're married?"

Rose pressed her lips together. "What do I have to do?"

"You were at Blake's wedding. You saw the way Laura

and Henrietta and Amanda all acted toward their husbands."

"They were all sweet and solicitous," Rose said. "Same as the men acted toward them."

Her words were a challenge if Bishop had ever heard one. "You think I can't act all caring toward a lady?"

"Kind of doubt it. Sure haven't seen any evidence of it yet." She tilted her chin in that haughty way of hers. "Got any experience with the ladies, Bishop?"

"I've known lots of ladies."

"I don't mean the kind where you leave the money on the night stand afterward."

In spite of himself, Bishop felt his face grow warm. "How do you even know about such things?"

"I bet I know more than you do when it comes to how things are between a man and a woman."

"Oh, yeah!" Bishop never could resist a challenge. And Rose was proving herself a handful in a dozen different ways. Impulsively he leaned in close, slid his arms around her middle and kissed her.

He figured he caught her off guard, because she started to open her mouth in a surprised gasp just as his lips found hers. He took full advantage of her parted lips to slide his tongue inside her mouth, slow and coaxing. Patiently he shaped and reshaped his lips to hers, enjoying the easy way they fit together as he engaged her tongue in a mutual exploration as old as time.

She must have liked it. He felt her hands on his shoulders holding him close as her lips softened under his. She made a breathy, sighing sound in the back of her throat that heated his blood as he deepened the kiss, pulling her closer so her bosom cradled his chest.

She was all woman, all right.

He was thoroughly enjoying the entire experience of having her in his arms and missed the signs she wasn't until her fingers dug into his shoulders like claws. She pushed him back so hard he nearly fell out of the wagon.

She wiped her mouth with the back of her hand. "That was disgusting," she hissed. "Decent folks don't kiss that way."

He smiled and tilted her chin between his thumb and forefinger quite certain his had been her very first kiss, and one she'd never forget. "Oh, yes they do, Rose. All that and a whole lot more."

She spun away and turned her back as if she couldn't bear to look at him.

"Just remember," he said, "you came to us. There's going to be a whole lot more playacting required before we best Hawkes."

As she clambered down from the wagon Rose heard what Bishop said about playacting loud and clear. She'd turned away because she needed to hide her smile lest she give herself away. If a few kisses were all it took to have him dance to her bidding, it was a small price to pay.

Truth be told, she'd liked everything about the kiss— from his touch to his lips on hers to the warm intimacy of his tongue lapping against hers and the way his breath filled her lungs. He felt good and smelled even better.

She planned to have him kiss her again, and often. Bishop had no idea the skill level of playacting she had reached as she matured. Pretending to be someone else was the only way she had survived this long.

She rounded the front of the wagon and linked her arm

companionably through his. "All right, husband dearest. What's next?"

She was pleased to see the way his jaw dropped and his eyes narrowed. Throwing Bishop off balance was going to be fun. She just had to be careful it didn't distract her from her true mission. Finding Lily.

"When we go inside I'll introduce you to Smitty, the store proprietor. Let him know we'll set up for some book lending. Tell him we've got mail for a few folks. Find out if any strangers have been through town. What's your sister look like?"

"She's fair."

"Hair your color?" He ran his hand through the escaped strands of her braid as if he had every right to do so. The pads of his fingers grazed her scalp in a way that sent tingles up and down her neck and as far as her bosom in the front. Suddenly she felt flushed.

"More fair," she said. Her own hair was the color of darkened honey. Her sister's was like spun gold or liquid sunshine.

"Good."

"Good how?"

"A lady with light-colored hair is bound to stick out. Most of the folks hereabouts have dark hair."

Rose nodded. She hadn't thought about it before, but for families who had lived in the area a long time, there had likely been some mixing of blood with both the Mexicans and the Indians through the years.

"Unfortunately, it will also make her more valuable. If he intends to sell her, that is. Some men would pay big coin to have themselves a fair-haired trophy to show off."

Rose shuddered at the thought.

Bishop must have felt the terror his words kindled, for

his other hand gentled on her arm. "We'll find her, Rose. Barron and I are good at this kind of stuff."

She nodded and swallowed thickly as they made their way inside the store.

"Morning, Smitty," he called out.

An older, bespectacled gent appeared from behind a curtain, wiping his hands on a cloth. "It's afternoon," he said, glowering in a way that led Rose to suspect they had interrupted his midday meal.

Bishop shrugged. Rose wondered if that was his idea of an apology.

She turned to Bishop. "Sweetheart," she cooed. "The poor man was likely enjoying a break. Perhaps we should come back later."

She saw the shop owner's demeanor change immediately. "I never could tell you boys apart. Who's this lovely lady on your arm?"

"This here is my wife Rose," Bishop said.

Smitty nodded. "Heard tell there's been more weddings in Bullet lately than a body can shake a stick at. Your brother get himself hitched as well?"

"Not yet," Bishop said. "Bets are he'll be next. We left him behind this trip because—" He leaned in and gave the man a bawdy wink. "Being newlyweds and all, we need our privacy."

The man's snicker came out more like a snort. "I bet you do. How long you fixing to stay?"

"Just one night," Bishop said. "Can you help spread the word to folks if they need some new books? I fetched some mail for here from the post office in Yuma when we were passing through."

"I can take the mail," Smitty said. "Know everybody in these parts."

"I know you do," Bishop said in a casual way. "Any new faces been through lately?"

"Travel through is all folks do these days," Smitty said with a downtrodden look. "Got no ken to stay. Everyone's looking for the next big strike. Out west. Up north. Anyplace but here."

"The church ladies still having their meetings? Rose here was just saying how she misses the womanly chats she was accustomed to before we got married."

"They won't be at the church today," Smitty said. "On account of it's pickling day over at old Mrs. Wagner's place."

"Pickling day?" Bishop turned to Rose, his face alight with held-back laughter. "You hear that, sweetheart? This is your chance to go help the ladies with their pickling."

Rose batted her eyes at him at the same time she ground the heel of her boot against his instep. No way he was getting rid of her to go slave over a hot stove making pickles with a bunch of the town biddies.

"Oh, darling. I couldn't possibly leave you to tend the book wagon all on your own. Besides," she stroked his arm in an adoring fashion. "I can't bear for us to be separated more than a minute."

As she spoke, she smiled over at Smitty, who was closely watching the proceedings. She knew it would take no time at all for word to spread about the arrival of the young couple with the book wagon.

"Do you know what it's like to be newlywed, Mr. Smitty?"

"'Fraid I'm a bachelor, ma'am. But I can do some imagining."

Rose rocked up onto her tiptoes and pressed a kiss to Bishop's cheek. She could feel the beginning of the day's growth of whiskers under her lips. "The real thing is far more fun."

Bishop cleared his throat and unwrapped Rose's arm from his. "I'll just go fetch that mail, Smitty. You wait here a sec, pumpkin?"

"Hurry back, darling." Rose waggled her fingers in what she hoped was a coquettish fashion.

The second Bishop was gone, Smitty leaned across the counter. "Which twin did you wind up marrying?"

"Oh, that's Bishop," she said. "Barron's a little too rambunctious for me."

"They ever pull one over on you? Or try to? Used to do that all the time around here."

Rose twinkled. "Not that I know for sure. But wouldn't that be just deliciously naughty of them if they did?"

Smitty blanched, then guffawed and slapped his knee.

Bishop reappeared with a small bundle of mail, which he placed on the counter, glancing from Smitty to Rose and back again with a puzzled look.

"Something funny?"

"This bride of yours, Bishop. Very funny gal."

"Rose's sense of humor is what first attracted me to her," Bishop said, but there was wariness in the way his eyes rested on her. He must have a sense she was up to something, but just wasn't sure what. Rose loved it!

"You setting up the wagon in the usual spot by the river?" Smitty asked.

"That's right," Bishop said. "I take it there are no new ladies hereabouts close to Rose's age, case she's in the mind for a little womanly company later?"

Smitty gave his head a shake. "Maybe if there was, I wouldn't still be a bachelor."

The second they were out the door, Rose turned on him.

"Why are we staying?" she hissed. "You heard him. There's no one here that could be Lily. We should be moving on to the next town."

Bishop shook his head. "Gotta stick to the usual routine. Set up and greet the folks and swap out their books. Besides, you never know what you might find out talking to the townsfolk."

"Like the pickle ladies?" Rose said, crossing her arms over her chest. "Find out which kind of vinegar they prefer?"

Bishop shook his head and tugged on her braid. "What did you say to old Smitty back there while I was fetching the mail? Never seen him quite like that before."

"Nothing much," Rose said innocently. "Just chit chat."

Bishop gave her another one of those looks that stopped her heart before sending it racing. "Don't kid a kidder, Rose. And whatever you do, don't try to con a conner."

They weren't the only wagon with a mind to set up near the river. They drove past a colorful caravan that had arrived ahead of them, festooned with garish signs proclaiming the owner held the secret elixir to happiness and health. A second sign promised fortune-telling and visits from one's relatives who had passed.

"Snake oil," Bishop muttered as he drove past, careful to keep a wide swath between the self-proclaimed fortune-teller and themselves.

Rose had never come across anything like it in her travels. "You think it's on the up and up?" she said. "Telling fortunes and curing ills?'

Bishop blinked at her as he drew the wagon to a stop. "Wanna buy a bridge?"

She frowned. "I don't understand. You can't buy a bridge."

"And you can't tell the future or cure a broken heart with

a vial of snake oil." He snorted. "Folks thought Barron and I ran a con. It was nothing compared to this guy."

"Do you know him?"

"Only by reputation. Brody hates his kind on account of his ma ran off with someone just like him. Left Brody alone with his pa, who wasn't much of a father. Used to leave Brody outside the saloon for hours on end while he was inside gambling."

"Is that how Brody became a gambler as well?"

"Brody's one of us."

"One of us?"

"Someone who does whatever it takes to survive. Come help me get this set up. It won't be long before folks find out that we're here."

Rose noted the way Bishop took care of the horses first, removing their traces and feeding them. Only then did he open up the side wall of the book wagon so folks could see inside.

"See how each book has a card inside?" he said. "This box of cards here at the end of the shelf is for the books that are already out on loan. Folks bring back a book, you fetch its card, note the date it was returned, slip the card back inside and put it on the shelf. Storm has it pretty organized. History and science here. Dime novels up there. Fairytales over there. Love stories here. What she calls the classics are up there. You'll figure it out. Don't worry if you mess it up. Barron and I do all the time."

"Seems pretty straightforward," Rose said. "If they ask for a book, I fill out the card with their name and date and file it in the box, right?"

"One other thing. This ledger is what Storm calls her 'black list'. That's folks who are always borrowing books but not returning 'em. If it happens too often, she won't lend them any more until they bring back the ones they already have. Most times it's just a matter of they lent it to someone else before she got back this way. Then she just changes the name on the card. But there's always someone who has no respect for books and doesn't deserve to borrow them."

"I wish she'd have come by when I was growing up," Rose said. "Look at all these books."

"See now why we didn't take too kindly when you tried to steal this rig?"

Rose swallowed thickly. "I'm sorry about that. But like you said, just doing what it takes to survive."

Bishop looked up. "And something else I just said. How it doesn't take long for word to get around town."

Rose followed his gaze to where a woman marched their way, dragging a string of children behind her. She counted seven, including the baby the oldest girl carried on one hip.

The woman gave Rose a tired smile as she passed several books through the open window to where Rose stood inside. "Do you have anything by Mark Twain?" the woman asked. "I've already read *Tom Sawyer*."

Rose's gaze flew to Bishop.

"You read *Huck Finn* yet?" he asked, finding it easily on the shelf.

"Not yet. Thank you," she said. "And the girls want to read *Little Women*."

"Got that right here."

While Bishop fetched the other book, Rose found the cards for the books the woman returned. "Mrs. Taylor. Is that right?"

At the woman's nod, she said, "I'll just note down here that these were returned. And write your name on the cards for the ones you're borrowing today."

The woman's face lit up with heartfelt thanks as Rose

passed her the books. "God bless," she said. "You truly are doing the Lord's work."

Rose thought about the extreme preachings of her father, filled with threats and punishing darkness and hellfire, truly believing he was doing the Lord's work. She much preferred this way. What a good feeling to make someone happy and brighten their day.

Others quickly took Mrs. Taylor's place at the lending window, and Rose was surprised at how busy they were. Dusk fell without her noticing before their trade slowed down.

"Is it always like that?" she asked Bishop, once the customers had tapered off and they were outside the wagon starting a fire to cook their evening meal. The fortune-telling wagon was still there, his fire a beacon in the dusk.

"Not always," Bishop said. "But busy enough that Storm is happy Barron and I are filling in for now." He straightened up from the fire and smiled down at her. "You and I make a good team. And your lettering is a lot better than Barron's."

"Bishop, I—" She bit off her words. What was she intending to say? He was sure to get the wrong idea if she said she was glad to be here. How she enjoyed working at his side. Or the charge she got out of seeing the way folks' eyes lit up when they got their hands on a book they wanted to read.

She'd never experienced the chance to do something nice for folks before now.

"I know," he said, his hands gentle on her shoulders, his voice low and intimate, as if they were the only two around for miles. "It gives you a good feeling, doesn't it?"

She bit her lip and looked down. "I feel different. Helping folks. It's new to me and—" How could she be so jumbled up inside? She shouldn't be enjoying herself. She shouldn't be happy here in Bishop's company. She hadn't thought about Lily for hours now and that was all wrong.

One of Bishop's hands slid from her shoulder to her jaw, then around the back of her neck.

He was going to kiss her again.

And much as she wanted to recapture that magic of his lips on hers, she needed to regain the upper hand. The kissing needed to be on her terms, not his.

Before she had a chance to move, the moment was interrupted by the sound of someone nearby clearing their throat in a noisy fashion.

Rose jumped back from Bishop and turned to see a dark-haired stranger watching them. He was dressed like no one she had ever seen, in a billowing white shirt, tight black breeches, with his dark hair falling loose past his shoulders.

"Sorry to interrupt." His voice was smooth and melodic. "I just came to offer my fire to cook your evening meal should you wish. Save you the bother of making one here."

She felt the way Bishop stiffened in a confrontational manner, his right hand instinctively heading for his weapon.

When the stranger's eyes met Rose's she couldn't look away. His gaze drew her in, spoke to her without words, as if he saw right through her and knew what was in her heart. She felt an unexplainable shiver. Not fear or excitement or revulsion but a powerful pull, the same way she was drawn to the moon when it was full, unable to look away.

"No thanks," Bishop said curtly. "We prefer our own company and our own kind."

"I understand," the man said, but he continued to move toward

Rose, never taking his eyes from hers. "I see her," he said.

"See who?" Rose asked, even though she already knew the answer.

"The woman you seek."

"That's enough." Bishop stepped forward threateningly. "Stay back, Rose."

"No, wait." Rose's arm shot out to hold Bishop back. "I want to hear what he has to say."

"Rose." Her name sounded different on the strange man's tongue. The way she imagined a rose would smell. Although she had never been close to one, she had seen pictures. "Your sister also has the name of a flower."

CHAPTER 6

From the corner of his eye, Bishop saw Rose freeze in shock. "Rose, he's nothing but a shyster."

Bishop didn't know if he was more irritated by the fact that the man had interrupted them just as he was about to kiss Rose, or the fact that she was getting hoodwinked by the charlatan.

"Her hair is the color of sunshine," the man continued. "She hears much but speaks not at all."

"What the hell is that supposed to mean?" Bishop asked.

The man shrugged. "Your voice has scared her away." He ignored Bishop and turned to face Rose. "When I saw her, she was filled with sorrow, her eyes overflowing with tears. She hates knowing that you are worried."

"Where is she?" Rose came to life and tugged at the man's arm. "Tell me where she is."

"That, alas, I do not know." He looked over to Bishop. "I did not mean to raise your hostility."

"Go peddle your snake oil someplace else," Bishop said. He locked eyes with the other fellow for several long beats before the man turned and melted into the darkness.

"Whoo whee!" Barron picked that moment to round the wagon and make his way toward them. "Don't believe a word he just said, Rose. Those guys operate that way."

"Kind of like you two?" Rose snapped.

Barron ignored her. "Thought for sure you'd have the fire going by now, with my meal ready and waiting."

"We've been busy," Bishop said shortly. "What took you?"

"Checking out the ladies like you told me. Most of them don't start working until later."

"There's not that many houses around here."

"Nope. But there sure are a lot of lonely ladies."

Rose interrupted. "He knew my sister's name."

Bishop cocked his head toward Barron who had squatted down, taking over the job of lighting the fire that Bishop had set up earlier. "Probably heard this big mouth here asking after her. Wouldn't take much to put two and two together."

"He knew the color of her hair."

"Lucky guess," Bishop said. "You're fair. Stands to reason she would be as well."

Flames crackled as the brush and twigs caught. Barron stood. "That reminds me. The steam boat's due in about an hour. That's where we need to be."

"Why?" Rose asked. "Did you find out something about my sister traveling by boat?"

"One of the girls thought she saw someone a few weeks back who might have been the lady I was asking about. Gal I chatted with was down at the dock to meet a fancy gent she was expecting. Her fancy fella never arrived, but she happened to see a rough-looking man with a young gal she'd not seen around town before. They arrived in town after dark and headed straight over to the boat. Which is why no one else saw her. Did anyone think to grab some vittles from the ranch house before we left this morning?"

"Laura sent some smoked ham to fry up, along with some new potatoes," Bishop said.

"I'm not hungry," Rose said. She turned and went inside the wagon.

Barron gave Bishop a knowing look. "Why do I get the feeling you did something to get our little friend in a bit of a dander?"

"It wasn't me," Bishop said. "It was that gypsy fortune-teller guy."

"You should have got the fortune-teller to spill the goods on Hawkes. What we need to do to see his days are numbered."

HAWKES RUMMAGED THROUGH THE BUNKHOUSE, not quite sure what he was looking for. He turned over mattresses and dug through kitbags, disgusted the entire time by the filth he encountered. How did men live like this? Earlier today he'd sent Denim and Haywire away on a trumped-up job in Yuma that should keep them busy all day.

Spies had reported seeing Haywire in Yuma a short time ago flashing a sizable wad of cash. And since Hawkes had yet to pay him what he was owed...

Hawkes put everything back the way he'd found it, not that it should make much difference. The men were so messy they'd likely never notice if their things had been rifled through or not. He'd turned to leave when a glint of sunlight came through the dirt-encrusted window pane and illuminated a slight chink in one of the floorboards near the window.

He dropped to his knees, fished out the knife he wore everywhere and managed to pry up the loose board. Underneath was a cubby hole with a dirty cloth wadded into it. Carefully Hawkes eased out the small bundle. He'd known something was going on ever since he heard about Haywire flaunting more money than a man like him should have access to. He'd bet his last dime those bastards had been stealing from him, striking out on their own and pulling heists he ought to be cut in on. Ingrates! And after all he'd done for them.

His hands shook as he unrolled the dirty chunk of canvas. Inside was a money pouch. Heavy from the feel of it. He opened it up and could hardly believe his eyes. Where had those bastards got their hands on this much money? He placed the pouch in his pocket, bundled up the canvas and stuffed it back into the cubby before he carefully replaced the floorboard. Then he went back to the ranch house to wait for their return.

ROSE STEPPED around the bedrolls and other clutter in the back of the book wagon and climbed the ladder up into the sleeping loft. How could her life be in such turmoil?

For months now, she had been focused on one thing and one thing only, finding her sister, and it sounded like she was getting close. Whether she listened to that charlatan or to Barron's story about the steamship passengers, she ought to feel relieved that the nightmare could be over soon.

So why did she feel like a worse dream was about to begin?

She'd seen enough lately to know she could never return to the life with her parents, but she had to accept that Lily might not feel the same way. Her sister had always been more timid, more drawn into herself, more subservient than Rose was. Lord only knew what Lily had been through lately, but she well might prefer to return to the comfort and familiarity of her old life.

Rose couldn't remember a time without her sister. The girls had been born less than a year apart, almost twins. She bit back a rueful smile. Scratch that. Barron and Bishop were the true twins. She and Lily were merely sisters, and very different from each other in the bargain. As were Bishop and Barron.

She knotted her hands together in her lap. She only prayed they found Lily soon and unharmed. Was that too much to ask? That her sweet, innocent sister, who would never harm a hair on anyone's head be unscathed by her ordeal.

It would be comforting if she was able to believe some of her father's preaching, that the Lord would take care of innocent folks like Lily. But she'd seen enough in her travels lately to not believe a word.

Bishop appeared at the wagon's door with a lantern in one hand and a plate in the other. "It's not good, you sitting here alone in the dark."

"I didn't notice," Rose said. "I was thinking about stuff."

Bishop set the lantern down on a small crate that doubled as a table and passed her the plate. "You said you weren't hungry, but you need to eat something."

"Thank you. That was most thoughtful." Her stomach rumbled at the smell of fresh ham as she clambered down the ladder and took the plate he extended.

"You shouldn't let yourself get rattled by what folks like that fortune teller have to say. Best see things for yourself and draw your own conclusions."

Rose bit back a smile as she slowly chewed a chunk of ham. "I guess you know what you're talking about on account of the cons you and your brother used to pull. Weren't you two kind of like that other fellow, only different? Selling people hope at the same time you bust up their dreams?"

Bishop stared down at his hands as if he didn't like what he was hearing before he squared his shoulders and met her gaze straight on. "I know you've grown up kind of sheltered and had to find out fast and hard about the real world, but you'll learn it's best you don't judge folks until you know firsthand just what they've been through and how they feel about things."

He turned to leave.

"Bishop, wait." Rose reached out and caught his arm to stop him from going. She set down her plate so both hands were free. "You're right. I have no right to judge others without knowing their story."

"You'd do well to remember that," Bishop said. "On account of how things might be when we find your sister."

"What do you mean?"

He pressed his lips together as if deciding how much to say. "Just warning you. There's a good chance she's seen and done some things she might not normally be part of. Done whatever she had to do in order to survive. Same like you when you were out there all alone trying to find her. You knew her before, but she might seem like a total stranger when we find her."

Rose felt her legs threaten to give way beneath her. Bishop must have known because she found herself in his arms, reassured by the strength of his hold. Feeling safe in a way she'd never been safe before.

She stroked his jaw with her fingertips, unable to tear

her eyes from his. She could see her own reflection mirrored in their depths. "How did things get so confused? I feel like I don't even know which way is up anymore."

He blew out a breath, and she felt its warmth filter through her hair doing delicious things to her scalp. She felt his heart thud heavily in his chest, and her own heart sped up as if trying to keep pace with his.

"Most of us feel like that every single day. We just don't think on it enough to let it get to us."

"I guess I've always had too much time to think."

The slow awakening of his smile lit up his face and did funny things to her insides.

"I've noticed lately, ever since my family started to change with first Brody getting married and then the others, that ladies seem to think differently from the way we menfolk tend to think on things."

She shifted closer until they were joined, thigh to thigh, hip to hip. She drew a deep breath. He smelled delicious. Leather and horses and fresh air. "Even I, in my somewhat sheltered life, know that!"

"We fellas are a little slower when it comes to certain things."

She spared him a teasing smile. "I know that as well."

He gave her a light tap on her bottom that turned into a soft caress. "Think you're smart, don't you?"

"I know I'm smart."

"Smart enough to know what'll happen if you stand here close to me any longer?"

"That too." Closing her eyes, she anticipated his kiss.

And he made her wait, drat him!

She opened her mouth in protest, just in time for his lips to swoop in and claim hers. Her tongue immediately danced with his before she traced the shape of his lips, found the harder ridges of his teeth, and inhaled deeply his taste and his essence.

She tangled her fingers through his hair, holding him in place, feeling like she could never get enough. This man. This embrace. This kiss.

She was suddenly ravenous for more, ravenous for everything. Heat bolted through her limbs, melting her with need. She felt boneless. Liquid. Like honey softened in the sun. And still she wanted more.

"Whoa!"

Abruptly Bishop ended the kiss, leaving her feeling dizzy and breathless.

She cocked her head and studied him in the dim lantern light. His chest heaved as he fought for breath. His pupils were dilated. Clearly he was as affected as she was, only trying to pretend otherwise.

He tucked in his shirt, which had somehow come untucked, and pointed to her meal plate. "You'd best finish that up. Then we'll head over to the steamship office. Boat's due in soon."

She was pleased to note his gait was slightly unsteady as he left.

BARRON LOOKED his way as Bishop stumbled out of the wagon and found his footing.

"Don't say a thing," he warned his twin.

Barron smirked. "You mean like don't be falling for those big, sad, rescue-me eyes?'

"Yeah, like that," Bishop mumbled.

"And for sure don't be buying the damsel-in-distress act?" Barron continued to goad him.

Bishop narrowed his gaze. "Rose is no more a damsel in distress than you or I. Remember when she tried to pick my pocket?"

"Not likely to forget," Barron said, as he scraped the uneaten bits of ham fat from his plate into the fire. "But here I see her playing you like one of those screechy violins."

"Violins aren't screechy."

"They are when they're not played right. And much as she's trying to play you, she doesn't have the right touch."

Man, was Barron wrong.

Rose had exactly the right touch to hit every scrap of nerve he tried to keep covered up. Caring. Sympathy. Empathy. Protectiveness. And something more. Something he tried to tell himself was pure lust but felt different.

"You think she's as good as her word?" Barron said. "To help us set up Hawkes for his final fall?"

Bishop thought on that. Was Rose as good as her promise?

Or was she like every other woman who said one thing and did another?

TIRED OF WAITING ALONE at the ranch house, Hawkes was pacing in the bunkhouse when Denim finally rolled in, followed by Haywire.

"What have you boys been up to?" he asked.

"Doing like you told us. Watching Fizzler's office. Might have helped if we knew what we were looking for."

Hawkes blinked at the two men, allowing the silence to

stretch between them. Letting them feel the full weight of his displeasure. "You questioning my authority?"

"No, boss," Denim said quickly.

"What about you, Haywire? Anything you been up to I should know about?"

Haywire looked like an owl caught up in the sunshine—facing something he neither liked nor was comfortable with.

Haywire shrugged his meaty shoulders. "Can't think what that might be."

"'Cause I can't help but wonder. Man like you, fresh out of prison. Still waiting on his first pay. Yet somehow you seem to have yourself quite a cache." He pulled out the money pouch and waved it in front of their faces. "You know anything about this?"

Denim shook his head, wide-eyed, as his gaze slid sideways to Haywire.

"Hey!" Haywire said, reaching for it. "That's mine. Earned it fair and square."

"Interesting." Hawkes stared at the pouch clenched in his fist, just beyond Haywire's reach. "'Cause I'd give my left nut to know just exactly what you did to earn this kind of cash. You work for me, remember?"

A stream of spittle slipped from one corner of Haywire's mouth. "It were before I came here."

"Do tell," Hawkes continued, as he rolled the money bag around in his palm.

"Up north, when I first got out of prison. Me and the other cons came across a bunch of Injuns. Had us some fun with them. We were setting to leave when along comes one of them crazy preacher fellas with his family. Snatched me up a pretty little fair-haired gal. Was damn sure the old man wouldn't have the balls to come after me, and I was right.

She was a surly little bitch, though. Couldn't wait to unload her."

"I take it you found a wealthy benefactor willing to trade you this purse for the girl?"

Haywire's head bobbed like a puppet on a string. "That's it. That's exactly how it happened. Good riddance, I said. Let the wench be someone else's problem."

Hawkes nodded as he digested Haywire's words. "Good work," he said. "I might need you to be doing that again for me real soon."

"Sure, boss." Haywire's throat seemed to swell as he swallowed a breath. "Can I have my money back?"

"This?" Hawkes stared down at the money pouch he held, as if seeing it for the first time. "Nah. I'm holding this against the room and board you owe me for all the time you been living here."

"But—" Haywire closed his mouth with a snap at the look Hawkes shot him.

Hawkes tucked the money pouch in his pocket, pausing at the doorway to speak over his shoulder. "Nice having this little chat, boys."

He headed back to the ranch house, whistling as he went.

BISHOP AND ROSE left Barron behind to keep an eye on the book wagon as they made the short walk through town to the steamship office. Neither spoke. One time Rose stumbled on the uneven ground and tensed when she found her hand caught and held tight in Bishop's grip. Slowly she relaxed as the warmth of his hand seeped into hers. She felt the unexpected reassurance wrought by his presence. It felt nice to no longer be chasing after her sister alone.

As they drew close, the smell of the river, damp and weedy, grew stronger. Torches illuminated the dock as the steamship slowed and pulled in. Behind the vessel, the river lay in darkness that her gaze was unable to pierce, but she could hear the movement of the water.

To her surprise, Barron didn't release her as they stood and waited while the mate secured the lines to the wharf. Rose jiggled with impatience as the gangplank was lowered to discharge a handful of the passengers coming back from Yuma. Last off was the ship's crew.

With Rose's hand still clasped in his, Barron stepped in front of a man wearing the uniform of captain. "Captain, a word if you please?"

"What is it?" The man frowned his impatience at being delayed.

"We're just wondering if you might have noticed a young lady on board in the last few weeks."

"Not many women on board these days."

"The one we're seeking would be hard to miss as she has unusually fair hair. Probably didn't look very happy with the company she was in. Maybe even being held against her will."

"Don't recall seeing anyone matching that description." Impatiently, the Captain continued on his way.

The last man to disembark was the purser, who slowed as he reached them, shifty eyes moving left to right.

"This lady you're looking for. Any chance there's a reward for information about her?"

Rose's heart leapt into her throat.

"You know where my sister is?"

Bishop tugged on her hand to signal she stay quiet.

"Depends what you know."

"Information has a price tag," the other fellow said with a shrug and prepared to move on.

Bishop met Rose's gaze. He reached into his pocket and removed a few bills. "Half now for what you know. You get the other half if the information proves good."

Their informant licked his lips in a furtive gesture and snatched the bills out of Bishop's hand.

"Lady like you describe was on board a few weeks back. I remember her because she didn't look like she belonged with her companion. The man she was with smelled as bad as he looked."

Rose let out a gasp of dismay, only to feel the comfort of Bishop's arm slide around her shoulder.

"Anyone you know?"

"Never seen either of 'em before. I remember there was something funny about her. Never heard a word come out of her mouth, even when the other passengers spoke to her. Kind of thought maybe she was a deaf-mute or something. And that's why the man kept her so close to his side."

Bishop gave Rose a questioning look. She shook her head. It was true Lily had never been overly talkative, but she was certainly able to converse when she had something to say.

"You remember where they get off?" Bishop asked.

"Sure do. They left the ship at Yuma. Almost missed seeing them leave because so many folks were rushing to catch the train."

Rose slumped beneath Bishop's touch. "So they could have gotten on the train and gone anywhere."

"True enough," the other man said. "But the gal was kind of hard to miss. Maybe the ticket agent at the railway knows where they were headed."

"Thanks," Bishop said.

"Hey, what about the other half of the money?" the man whined.

"Afraid half the story only warrants half the money," Bishop said, clapping the other man on the back. "Appreciate you telling us what you know."

"I'll pay you back," Rose said, as they made their way back to their makeshift camp.

"Won't be necessary," Bishop said in smug tones.

"I insist," Rose said stubbornly. She had no intention of being beholden to Bishop or anyone else on this mission of hers. "My sister. My responsibility."

"And if I tell you I already reclaimed the money I paid him?"

She stopped and turned to stare at him. "You picked his pocket? I never saw a thing."

Bishop shrugged. "A well-honed talent."

"No wonder you caught me out when I tried that on you." She gave him a hopeful look. "Will you teach me?"

Bishop gave her a gentle prod in the direction of their camp, where the embers of the fire glowed against the dark night sky. "I will not."

She pushed out her bottom lip. "Spoil-sport."

"You've got enough tricks up your sleeve without adding a gift for thieving into the mix."

She jutted her chin at him, struck by his words. "I'm not sure what you mean."

He tugged lightly on her braid as they reached the book wagon. "Sure you do, Rose. You keep changing tactics in an effort to trip me up. But I'm on to you. Got a feeling those folks who travel around the territory putting on their stage performances have nothing on you. Good night."

"Where are you planning to sleep?" she asked suspiciously as he climbed into the wagon behind her.

He pulled out two bedrolls. "Barron and I will bunk down out by the fire. You get some rest."

She stared at his retreating back, trying to figure out how he came to know her so well on such short acquaintance.

CHAPTER 7

I t seemed to take twice as long to reach Yuma as it had when they traveled toward Castle Dome Landing. At least it felt that way to Rose, who once again found herself sandwiched between the twins, conscious of Bishop's shoulder jostling her at every pot-hole the wagon jounced over. Barron managed to stay on his side of the seat, unlike Bishop who, drove the horses. Which made her think he was doing it on purpose.

She'd lain awake most of the night, overthinking things the way she did. Unfortunately she now had even more thoughts chasing around in her brain. Including the sense that Bishop saw straight through her ploy.

How might he react when he found out she'd made him a promise she'd never be able to keep?

Finally, they reached their destination. Rose found a modicum of comfort in the familiar sights and sounds of Yuma as they left Barron at the train station to start making enquiries.

"Why can't I be the one asking after Lily?" Rose said.

Bishop looked at her and shook his head. "You know

what we were talking about earlier? About men and women thinking different from each other?"

She nodded.

"Well, they share information in a different way as well."

"What do you mean?"

He blew out a breath, as if to imply he really didn't feel like taking the time to explain something to her that was so obvious. "Say the ticket agent knows something but he holds back because he's afraid it might upset you."

"I don't follow," Rose said.

"Men treat women different. They talk different. Try to spare their sensibilities. Man-to-man talk is more likely to get the straight goods. Which is what we're after."

"That's hardly right!" Rose flounced back in her seat and crossed her arms over her chest.

"Not much is," Bishop said. "Now I'm going over to the saloon, see what I can find out. Ask if anyone has seen a fair-haired lady in these parts. Can I trust you to sit here like a good girl and not drive off into the yonder?"

"Where would I go?" Rose said in surly tones.

"You asked us to help you, Rose. You need to trust us that we know the best way to go about that."

"How about you open up the book window before you go? Maybe I can at least make myself useful lending out some books."

He narrowed his gaze. "Why do I think book lending is just a ploy to be asking folks if they've seen your sister?"

"Plain to see I can't get away with much where you're concerned," she said.

"Remember that," Bishop said. "Spare yourself the grief of trying." But as he spoke, he set things up like yesterday for the book lending.

Hah!

She smiled to herself as she watched his retreating back. If anything, Bishop's words acted as a challenge, not a deterrent.

Sure enough, the wagon wasn't long open for business before she had a small crowd gathered around wanting to know what books she had that were new. Unfortunately, she didn't know the answer to that question, or many of the other inquiries that came her way. Apparently, she couldn't even do this right without Bishop's help.

The line-up had dwindled down to nothing before a new lady approached. Looking at her close-up, Rose understood why she'd waited. For while she might not know much about book lending, she did recognize the type of female who stood at the window—, the kind of "fancy-lady" who worked in a house to entertain gentlemen.

Taking a closer look beneath the heavy make-up and what appeared to be a wig, she realized the woman in front of her was actually a girl, probably younger than Rose or Lily.

"Heard tell Storm got herself a husband over in Bullet." The gal's question was tinged by a wistful tone, and Rose reminded herself not to be quick to judge others. For all she knew, right now her sister could be in an identical situation to the young woman before her.

"That's right," Rose said in a friendly fashion. "Married herself one of the Mason brothers."

"Do you happen to know which one?"

"Blake Mason. You know him?" Rose asked curiously. Stood to reason the Mason bachelors could have frequented the house where this lady worked.

The other gal shook her head.

"Anything special you feel like reading?"

"It's not for me," the girl said. "I can't read much, not

enough to read a whole book or anything. But there's a gal I know. She keeps re-reading the same book over and over on account of it's the only one she has. She doesn't say much, but I thought she might like something new to read. If that's okay that it's not for me."

"That's perfectly fine," Rose said. "What is it your friend is reading?"

"It looks like a fairytale, by a writer with a funny name."

"Do you know what it's called?"

"I can write the letters. I don't know how you say it."

Rose passed over her pencil and a scrap of blank paper from the box of book cards. The girl's tongue peeked from between her parted lips as she labored over the letters.

"She must be a good friend if you're going to so much trouble to surprise her," Rose said kindly, as the girl scratched on the paper.

"Don't know her good," the girl said. She pushed the paper toward Rose. "I think that's right."

Undine!

Rose's mouth fell open as she stared in disbelief at the crudely formed letters before her. That very book had been Lily's most prized possession and was never out of reach, usually tucked inside the pocket of her apron. Both girls knew if their father found it, he would announce it as the work of the devil and see it was destroyed.

"Where is your friend now?" she asked, keeping her tone even so as not to startle the girl.

"She's ... She's at the house where we work."

"How about I pick out a few books and we take them over there now to see which ones she'd like to read?" Rose stood and pulled a few random titles haphazardly from the shelf behind her, her hands trembling with eagerness.

Lily! It had to be Lily!

BISHOP RAN into Barron coming from the train station. "Any luck?"

Barron shook his head. "No one seems to remember seeing a woman with fair hair getting on the train with a somewhat disheveled, disreputable companion."

"I've been telling folks how I have a book that a customer ordered," Bishop said. "Tried the general store, the post office, the hotel and the café to see if anyone knew where I could find her. No luck."

"What about the livery?" Barron asked. "Maybe they hired horses or a buggy?"

"Great idea. If they're not here in town, they had to have some form of transport to leave."

"It seems a lot of folks have been passing through lately," Barron said. "No word of anyone new in the last little while fixing to stay in the area."

"Why don't you go over to the bank? Maybe you can find out if anyone new has shown up there lately?" Bishop said. "I'll try the solicitor."

"Solicitor won't tell you anything," Barron said. "Client privilege and all that. Why don't you go see if anyone's up yet over at Zara's. I'll stop by the bank, then meet you there."

ROSE HAD her wits about her enough to close the window and lock the book wagon door before she followed her companion through the winding streets to a pretty house situated a short distance from the others at the end of a dead-end road.

Bishop would be fuming when he found out she'd just

left the wagon parked there with the horses hitched to it, but she didn't care. Any minute now, she'd see Lily. She pushed any thoughts from her mind as to what kind of house her sister was working in, or what kind of life she might have been forced into.

When they reached the house, the girl didn't go in the front way but followed a weed-licked pathway around the house to the back porch. She pushed open the unlocked rear door, which led directly into the kitchen.

Even though it was past noon, half a dozen ladies clad in various items of nightwear sat around the table drinking coffee and yawning. Her new companion went right up to the girl seated on the end.

"Elsa," she said. "This here is the book lady who's taking over the lending wagon from Storm. She brought you some books."

Disappointment washed through Rose as the woman called Elsa looked up at her with a calculated look. "Didn't know you made house calls," she drawled. The familiar, well-thumbed version of *Undine* sat next to her saucer.

Rose walked over to her. "Where did you get the book you're reading?"

"This?" She gave the book in question a dismissive tap. "Relax. It's not one of yours."

The door behind Rose opened. "Found it in *her* room." Elsa inclined her head toward the newcomer.

"Lily!" Rose shrieked and raced across the room to enfold her sister in a bear hug.

Immediately she knew something was wrong. Not only did Lily not hug her back, she stood as stiff as a board in Rose's embrace.

Rose took a step back and gave her sister a scrutinizing look. "Lily. What's wrong?"

When there was no answer, she glared accusingly at the other women seated at the table. "What's wrong with her? What have you done to her?"

"What's all the hullabaloo?" An older woman came through the doorway Lily had just entered, rubbing her face with one hand and smearing her kohl eyeliner across her cheek. "Can't a body get any sleep?"

"It's her fault." Elsa pointed at Rose.

The older woman approached. "I'm Zara, and this is my establishment. I don't cotton to folks arriving and getting things all stirred up. Don't allow it from the gents. I certainly don't aim to see it from a chit of a girl like yourself."

Rose moved protectively to Lily, who was staring at her like she'd never seen her before. "Lily is my sister. I've been searching for her ever since she was kidnapped."

"Lily, huh?" Zara said, as she padded to the stove and poured herself a cup of coffee. "Never knew that was her name."

"What do you mean?" Rose asked.

"Hasn't said a word since she got here," Zara said. "It's like she's forgot how to speak. Right along with who she is and where she came from."

They were interrupted by a burly, finely-dressed gentleman with dark skin, who stuck his head through the door. "'Scuse me, Zara. A couple of the Mason boys are at the front door. Claim they need to see you on urgent business."

BISHOP NOTICED how different Zara's front parlor looked in the daylight.

"Think she'll agree to see us?" he said to Barron as they waited. "Seeing as how we're not here for personal reasons."

Barron touched his baby finger to a key on the piano in the far corner. "Sure, she will. If only because of Braydon having grown up here."

"Even Braydon doesn't use the front door during the day," said a familiar voice behind them. "Or touch the piano."

"Sorry, Zara." Bishop shot Barron a look. "We didn't know."

"What's so all-fired important that it can't wait till a decent hour?"

"Favor for a friend," Barron said. "She's looking for her sister who was kidnapped. Heard tell the sister was last seen headed this way. Figured if anyone knew anything, it would be you."

Zara's face pulled in a frown. "Is this some kind of joke?"

"No, ma'am. Dead serious," Bishop said.

"Then kindly explain to me why right at this exact moment, there's a woman in the kitchen making the same claim."

Bishop exchanged looks with Barron. "She's here now?"

How Rose knew anything about Zara's place, let alone found her way here was a mystery for another day.

"Thought you told her to stay put," Barron said to Bishop.

"Fat lot of good that did," Bishop muttered.

"What are you planning to do to make that woman ever listen?" Barron sneered.

"He's not going to do anything to anyone," Zara said in a no-nonsense tone. "You'd both better come through," she continued with a sigh. "Turns out that sister everyone is so het-up about finding is here as well. Don't know what happened to the poor thing, but she doesn't seem to have any memory. Doesn't even recall how to talk."

ROSE LOOKED up as the kitchen door opened to admit Zara, followed by Bishop and Barron, crowding the confines of the room. Without a word the other ladies rose en masse clutching their coffee cups, and left the room.

"So this is Lily?" Bishop asked, rocking back on his heels, hands stuffed in his pockets.

"Told you we'd find her," Barron said smugly to Rose.

Rose sighed and smoothed a tangled strand of Lily's flaxen hair behind her ear. "She doesn't remember me."

"How'd she come to be here, Zara?" Bishop asked their hostess who stood frowning at the proceedings, arms crossed over her saggy bosom.

"Some ex-con came by with her. Claimed he never touched her. Wanted to keep her in prime condition." Zara shrugged. "What can I say? I've got a soft heart. I couldn't leave her with him. Had no idea if she'd ever work out as one of the girls, but not a one of them ever gets forced into the life. For now I got her doing the laundry and cleaning and stuff. Hoped she'd start to feel safe here and get her voice back. Cause it's plain she can hear well enough." She directed her words toward Lily. "Isn't that right, Lily? I know you can hear us."

Lily's gaze skittled from one person in the kitchen to the other, as if unsure if she should dart away and hide.

Rose stepped protectively to Lily's side. "She's my sister. I've looked after her for her entire life. I can handle things from here."

"Not so fast," Zara said. "I've got a sizable investment in her."

Rose slumped, then straightened determinedly. "I have a job in Bullet. It'll take some time, but I'll pay you back. You have my word."

"Despite what certain church-going folks might think, I don't cotton with passing girls around like so much chattel," Zara said. "Decision will be Lily's if she goes with you or stays."

Zara stepped forward so she was face to face with Lily. "What do you say? This gal here claims to be kin. You want to go off with her, or stay here where folks have been kind?"

Rose held her breath as Lily's gaze slid from person to person in the room. She held a pleading hand toward her sister. "I've been looking for you for months. Surely, with me, you will eventually get back your memory."

Lily locked her gaze with Rose, raised her chin and shook her head. Deliberately she moved to Zara's side.

CHAPTER 8

Rose turned and left the kitchen before Lily could see the tears welling up in her eyes. By the time she navigated her way across the porch and down the back steps, she could hardly see where she was going.

"Rose, wait!"

Bishop caught up to her easily before she reached the street. She had no choice but to wait for him. She had no idea where she was or where she was going.

She dashed away her tears with the back of one hand and pressed her lips together tightly as she faced him.

For months now, she'd been consumed with finding her sister. Everything she did or thought centered solely around finding Lily. To once again have it be the two of them together. Not in her wildest imagining could she have foreseen this outcome. To locate her sister, only to have her overtures rebuffed. To witness with her own eyes Lily choosing a perfect stranger over her.

She looked up at Bishop. "What did I do? What horrible thing, real or imagined, would have her turn on me like that? To choose a stranger over me?"

Bishop took her arm gently, as if he sensed how fragile she was. "Barron went to get the book wagon."

He spoke as if he hadn't heard a single thing she just said.

"What am I supposed to do now? Finding Lily has been my everything. Even though she's been found, she might as well have stayed lost forever."

"Nothing's forever," Bishop said. "More'n' likely she just needs some time. What do you bet she wakes up one day soon and remembers everything? Zara will let her know where you are, and..."

"And what? She'll waltz into Bullet as if nothing happened? 'Sorry about that, Rose. I hope you weren't terribly inconvenienced by the time I was away. I hope you didn't put your whole life on hold or anything.'"

Bishop stared straight ahead. Eventually he cleared his throat noisily, as if it was choked up solid. "At least you know where she is. That she's okay, sort of."

"Would that be enough for you if it was Barron? Knowing where he was? Knowing he didn't remember you?"

"You want to stay here in Yuma so you're close?"

Rose shook her head. "I have no idea where I should go or what I should do next."

THE DRIVE back to Bullet was a quiet one. From time to time, Bishop snuck sideways glances toward Rose. Some of those times he saw a few stray tears glisten on her cheeks like fat raindrops, but she never made a sound.

A woman in tears was something Bishop had learned to run a million miles from, so he just urged the wagon as fast as the horses could manage. The sooner he got Rose back to

Bullet among the womenfolk, the better. At this point, he envied Barron, who had elected to pass the drive in the rear of the wagon, mumbling something about "straightening up back there."

"Well, here we are," he said in an overloud voice as he drew the wagon to a stop outside the café. He tried for an encouraging smile. "At least you know where Lily is. You can go visit. Maybe something will eventually happen to jog her memory."

"She doesn't want to remember," Rose said sadly. "This has always been Lily's way of coping. Going all quiet was her way of ignoring what went on."

Bishop straightened. "You mean she's done this before? Refused to talk?"

"A few times. Never lasted for long."

"What did your folks do?"

Rose blew out a breath. "Sometimes our father would intone to God to bring back her speech. Other times he'd punish her until she spoke."

Bishop felt bad memories threaten to crash in on him. "Punish her how?"

"Extra chores. Bread and water. Or force her to spend hours on her knees praying."

Bishop had no truck with relatives who were neither caring nor sympathetic. "Maybe she's afraid you'll do the same. Force her to talk."

"She doesn't remember me. She doesn't know who I am or what our life was like."

"Maybe," Bishop said, unconvinced. "Or maybe she remembers it all too well." He turned to Rose. "You going to be okay?"

His heart gave a hollow thud at the sad, defeated look in her eyes.

"I have absolutely no idea."

"Come out to the ranch," he said impulsively, although he could have bit his own tongue the second the words were out of his mouth.

"Thank you for the offer, but I'm afraid I'm hardly fit company."

Bishop squared his shoulders and urged the horses forward before Rose could try to get out. "Too bad. Barron and I held up our end of the bargain. Now it's time for you to hold up yours."

ROSE CLAMBERED down from the wagon when they arrived at the ranch, thinking how different this arrival was compared with last time when she'd been locked in the rear of the wagon after trying to steal it.

Around the back of the wagon she heard the twins discussing her in low voices, but her hearing was excellent, and she caught every word.

"Why'd you bring her back here?" That had to be Barron.

"I didn't think it was a good idea to leave her alone. She's had a big shock."

"Since when did you get all sensitive towards women and their feelings?" Barron again.

A remark Bishop obviously didn't dignify to answer. But Rose wondered the same thing. Why did he care how she felt?

"I expect the ladies will all be in the big house." Bishop rounded the wagon then took her arm and guided her to the front door as if he was afraid she might bolt.

Rose had met all the Mason brides at Storm and Blake's

wedding and then again at the christening, but she felt unaccountably shy as Bishop prodded her inside.

"I hope it's okay I invited Rose for supper," he announced to no one in particular.

"Of course," the four women chorused back as they all looked up from a sheaf of papers unrolled across a massive table in the center of the room.

"Goodness, is it that late already?" Henrietta straightened and began to re-roll whatever had them so engrossed.

"Not that late," Bishop said. "Whatcha got there?"

"Nothing really," Henrietta said quickly before she tied a satin ribbon around the roll.

"Bishop, go see how far out the others are, would you, please?" Laura spoke up. "Let them know the meal is going to be a bit late tonight."

Rose wondered what had the ladies so entranced that they'd lost track of time.

Amanda, who was clearly in a family way, took one look in Rose's direction, followed by a second. "Oh, my dear. Whatever happened? You look like you just lost your best friend."

Rose blinked back the sudden unwanted surge of moisture in her eyes. "Nuh... nothing happened."

Amanda took her hand kindly and urged her in the direction of the now clear table. "I hate to tell you this, but something about carrying new life has made my instincts razor-sharp."

The kindness in her voice was Rose's undoing.

"I think you know my sister was kidnapped a few months ago. Bishop and Barron have been kind enough to help me search for her. Earlier today we finally found her."

Henrietta let out a snort. "The twins are generally good

men. But if they agreed to help you, there was more than likely something they wanted from you in return."

Rose knotted her hands together. "I may have given them the impression that I'm in a position to help them in their feud against Hawkes."

Laura's head jerked sharply in her direction. "The men have more than a feud going with Hawkes."

Rose nodded. "I saw that at the christening."

Amanda sat down and urged Rose to take the chair next to her. "Are the twins cooking up something on their own?"

"We were talking about a possible plan. Once we found Lily."

"Brody won't like that," Laura said.

Amanda caught Rose's hand in her own. "The bad blood between the Masons and Hawkes is a complicated story that goes back to Brody's uncle's time. Maybe even earlier."

"No one is to retaliate against Hawkes without the sanction and the full cooperation of the others," Storm added. "They made a pact."

Rose felt her stomach tie into knots. "You can't tell anyone what I just said. The twins will blame me for betraying them, and I never would have found Lily without their help."

"Where is your sister now?" Amanda asked. "Because even though you found her, you don't seem happy about it."

"She's in Yuma. It appears she doesn't remember anything. Not even me."

"If that's the case, you must bring her here to be with you," Laura said. "Spending time with someone who knows her from the past could prove helpful with regaining her memory."

"I wanted to," Rose said. "But she chose to stay with that other woman."

"What other woman?" Amanda asked.

"The woman that the kidnapper sold Lily to. At one of those houses."

"And now this woman won't let her go? That's terrible," Storm said.

"I think she might if I pay her back. But it'll take me some time to save. The other thing is, I'm not sure Lily wants to remember about our family."

"Everyone wants to know where they came from," Amanda said. "I know that because so many of the brothers are orphans. This is the only family they know."

"Our childhood wasn't easy," Rose said. "Lily was far too sensitive for the life we had with our parents. I felt her slipping away even before the kidnapping."

"Who is this woman who has your sister?" Henrietta asked. "They're not all hardened from the life. Some of them are very kind."

"Her name is Zara."

The ladies all exchanged a long, silent glance.

Finally, Henrietta spoke. "Braydon should be able to talk to Zara on your behalf. I'll mention it to him as soon as I see him. Don't you worry. We'll have your sister back before you know it."

"Lily can be stubborn," Rose said. "Who knows what she's been through these past months?"

"You leave this to us," Henrietta said. "And now I could use a hand preparing dinner."

"I THINK this is one of your dumbest plans ever," Barron said. He and Bishop were on fresh mounts headed toward Yuma.

"No one made you come with me," Bishop said.

"Just remember, I was born first," Barron said. "Makes it my job to look after you."

"Need I remind you how many times I patched you up after a fight?" Bishop said.

"That's 'cause I didn't want you getting hurt in the ring."

While Barron loved to fight.

"Who says I would have gotten hurt? Maybe I would have been better than you."

They were halfway to Yuma when they met a trio of riders coming toward them, riding shoulder to shoulder. The oncoming riders refused to fall back or give way, nearly forcing Bishop and Barron off the road as they pulled up and waited for the trio to pass.

Once they were close enough to recognize the three-some, Bishop's gut clenched. His hands on the reins tightened into claws. A total wash of hatred filled his veins. One look at Barron told him his twin felt it too. For a brief second he thought there was going to be a standoff, right here, right now. Hawkes rode in the middle and once they were within spitting distance, looked right through them as if they didn't exist.

Once past, the two men flanking Hawkes turned and kept a watchful eye over their shoulders, their gaze only leaving the twins when they disappeared around a bend in the road.

"Hawkes must have himself a couple new lackeys," Barron said once the men were out of sight.

Bishop ground his teeth. "It galls me that he's just out riding around, strutting his stuff like he never killed Joe."

"We know he killed Joe. And he knows we know it. This isn't over until it's over," Barron said.

"And Hawkes is in the ground," Bishop said darkly.

ROSE COULDN'T STOP WATCHING the door as one by one, the Mason brothers arrived for the evening meal, wondering what to make of the fact that the twins were noticeably absent. Was it because she was here? Had Bishop dumped her with his family and taken off? If so, why?

She had the rest of the brothers pretty well sorted out, helped along by the fact that each man greeted his wife with an affectionate kiss. All except bachelor Benjamin. She knew which one he was from seeing him at the café from time to time, chatting to Georgina.

Brody's voice boomed through the room. "Anybody know where the twins are?"

There were a few murmurs of dissent.

"Shouldn't we wait a few minutes longer?" Laura said.

"Forget it," Benjamin said. "They've been caught up in their own agenda for a while now."

Rose noticed the way he and Brody locked gazes across the room. "Anything the rest of us ought to know about?" Brody asked.

"No family business at the table," Laura said briskly. "It's bad for digestion. Plus we have a guest. I suggest everyone start eating before the food gets cold."

Rose was impressed with the quiet, effective way Laura laid down the law. Brody might be the head of the family, but his wife was every bit as powerful in her own way. Such a difference from the way her parents had been. Her father was always bellowing at the top of his lungs, as if to ensure the Almighty heard him above the rest of the mortal masses. Her mother, on the other hand, rarely said a word.

Everyone had just started to dish up when there was a commotion outside.

"Sounds like they're back," Brody said to no one in particular.

"Told you it wasn't like them to miss a meal," Benjamin said as the door flew open.

Rose looked up and dropped her fork in shock. The twins filled the doorway. Dwarfed between the two men stood Lily. Before Rose could move, Laura was on her feet.

"You must be Rose's sister, Lily. We're so very glad you could join us." To Rose's surprise, Laura pressed a quick kiss to the cheek of each twin. "Good job fetching her here, boys. Rose has been quite worried."

Within seconds, an extra chair for Lily was slid in next to Rose. Bishop sat on Rose's other side, while Barron took a chair on the far side of Lily. Rose gave her sister a quick hug as everyone at the table resumed eating.

"It's okay," she said to Lily. "You'll be safe here."

Lily stared down at her plate as if she didn't quite know what it was for. On Lily's other side, Barron quickly loaded his own plate before he placed a serving on Lily's as well.

Rose turned to Bishop, who was chowing down as if he hadn't eaten in days. "I don't understand. How did you get her to come with you?"

"Mason charm," Bishop said.

Rose raised her brows skeptically, waiting for more.

He shrugged. "Zara's a business-woman. She had already figured out Lily wasn't about to join the fold and earn Zara back her initial investment. Once Barron and I convinced Zara to cut her losses, she told Lily there was no place for her at the house and that she was better off coming with us." He looked past Rose to her sister. "For some reason, she took a shine to Barron. Rode all the way here up front of him on his horse without a murmur of complaint."

"Has she said anything yet?"

Bishop shook his head and turned his attention back to his plate.

"Why, Bishop?"

"Why what?"

"Why'd you go back for her?"

Bishop took his time chewing and swallowing, as if framing his response. Before he could speak, Barron answered for him. "Figured as long as she stayed in Yuma, your mind would be on other things than what we discussed back when this all got started."

Rose didn't believe him. "Is that true, Bishop?"

"Barron and I. We got separated from our brother Joe, doing what he thought at the time was the right thing. Learned the hard way nothing good ever comes from family being separated."

Rose stared down at her nearly untouched meal, suddenly at a loss for words. Was that how Lily felt?

Eventually she cleared her throat. "Whatever you paid out to Zara, I'll pay you back."

His eyes found hers in that warm, intimate way he had of looking at her, as if they were the only two people in the room. "I know you will, Rose."

Tingles spread through her at his words. Bishop had come through for her in a way no one else could match. Not only had he helped her find Lily, but he had taken steps to ensure the sisters could be together.

She felt mildly ashamed when she considered how many times she had tried to put one over on him. First before they even met. And then again when they were at Castle Dome Landing. Bishop was right. Never try to con a conner.

He had moves she'd never see coming. And this latest with Lily was one of them.

How could he know her so well? Know what she needed? Know how she'd react?

Before she even knew herself.

"Georgina has been really good to me at the café. Do you think she'd allow Lily to work there as well?"

"Never hurts to ask."

Rose sat back and pushed away her half-eaten meal. Fresh guilt washed over her. For she was about to do something Bishop would never understand or forgive. Soon as she could manage it, she planned to take Lily and run.

CHAPTER 9

I t took some time, some thought and some planning, but at long last, one night after the café was closed, Rose packed a few things for herself and Lily, and they left town under cover of darkness. Rose felt somewhat guilty spending her meager savings, money that should by rights have gone to pay Bishop back, for the horse and supplies needed for the trip. But she justified necessity over nicety.

As she had thus far, Lily continued to do as she was told, moving woodenly, her face devoid of expression. No words passed her lips.

At least her sister wasn't one for complaining because Rose lost track of the number of long, hot days spent in the saddle before they finally came across their parents' encampment. The trip had been slow going because the two girls shared a single horse. Not being sure of Lily's frame of mind, Rose had been unwilling to give her sister her own mount in case, given the chance, Lily took off.

The closer they drew to the camp the more agitated Lily became. Where before she had sat still in front of Rose, she now began to flail around, frantically searching the surrounding countryside as if seeking a means of escape. He breathing grew ragged and jerky. Perhaps her sister's memory was starting to return, triggered by the familiar surroundings.

When they finally rode into sight, they received exactly the reception Rose expected. She and Lily might as well have been returning from a pleasant one-hour jaunt.

"Daughters," her father said. "Come and pray."

As usual, her mother simply watched from the sidelines, her hands knotted in her apron front, her eyes cast to the ground.

Rose dismounted first and walked directly up to her father. Lily slid from the saddle and remained next to the horse, as if it was the one familiar thing in her world.

"I will not pray with you," Rose hissed. "Not ever again."

"Blasphemy!" thundered her father.

"Do you know where I found Lily? Do you even care what happened to her?"

Her father's expressionless glance flitted toward Lily. "I will baptize her. Wash away whatever sins she may have incurred." He raised a threatening finger and waved it in Rose's face. "And you! You shall be punished for your disobedience. There is not enough penance to be done in your lifetime to atone for your sins."

From the corner of her eye, Rose watched her mother slowly make her way toward Lily, almost as if she was sleep-walking. She stopped less than an arm's length away and reached out to touch a strand of Lily's golden hair. To Rose's disbelief, Lily hauled off and smacked their mother across the face, knocking her to her knees.

"Come on, Rose," Lily yelled, as she leapt into the saddle. "Let's get the heck out of here!"

Rose stood frozen in shock.

"You heard her!" Seeming to appear from out of nowhere, Bishop galloped up alongside her.

Rose still hadn't moved before she was hauled onto his mount and plopped in front of him. He scooped up the reins, and the powerful horse wheeled around. Together they galloped from the camp on the heels of Lily and her mount. A short distance away, they caught up to Barron, who must have been keeping watch. Barron's mount fell into step next to Lily's.

Mentally and physically exhausted from the trip and what had just happened, Rose couldn't get out a single word. Surrendering to silence, she allowed herself to lean back against Bishop, gaining strength from his arms around her and the competent way he held the reins as he guided their mount on the heels of the other two.

Exhausted or not, she couldn't still the thoughts and questions darting through her head. One thing was for certain. Lily felt the same way she did about leaving behind the life they knew with their parents. She had hoped the familiar surroundings would trigger Lily's memory, but she hadn't expected them to render such shocking results.

"Lily spoke," she finally managed to say to Bishop as the miles widened between them and the camp.

"Figured she would eventually," Bishop said.

"I need to talk to her. Find out what she remembers. Get her to tell me exactly what happened."

"There's plenty of time for that," Bishop said. He inclined his head to where Barron and Lily rode ahead of them. "Barron will see that she finds her way to talking about things in her own way and her own time."

"How did you find us?"

"For someone who knows how to track, you're pretty unobservant about noticing when you're being followed."

"I meant what I said about paying you back," Rose said. "Every last dime."

"We've got a more important deal to be working on. Or did you forget?"

"I'm sorry I misled you," Rose said. "I have no kind of a plan to tackle Hawkes."

"That's okay. Barron and I do. We just need your and Lily's help."

"Laura said Brody would be mad if any of the family goes it alone."

"Yeah, well, by then it will be too late."

"Can we catch up to Lily? I have a lot of questions for her."

"Wait till we pitch camp. Give her some time to get used to all this in her own way."

It was well after dark by the time they stopped. In short order Bishop and Barron had a small fire going and a tent pitched. "You and Lily sleep in there," Bishop said. "Barron and I will take turns keeping watch."

And so it ended up with Rose and Lily sharing a bedroll the way they used to when they were young.

"It's nice to have you back." Rose didn't know what else to say. How to broach the myriad of questions that had been plaguing her all day?

As she spoke, she brushed and braided her sister's hair, the way she had when they were young. The familiar ritual, weaving the soft gold waves of Lily's fair hair into one thick yellow braid, made her want to cry. What happened to their childhood? Their innocence? Their trust?

"When did you get your memory back?"

"It started with bits and pieces, over the last short while," Lily said. "Today the entirety of it hit me like a tornado."

After Rose tied the end of the braid with a faded piece of pink satin ribbon, Lily lay down on her back and stared up at the roof of the tent. "Some of the fragments were so disjointed they made no sense. I wondered if I was only imagining part of what I thought I remembered. Or if I was losing my mind."

"That must have been scary," Rose said. "Did that man ... Did that man hurt you?"

Lily shook her head. "He was hard and rough. But I was glad he took me out of there. Glad he took me away."

"What?" Rose stared at her sister, open-mouthed, scarcely able to believe what she was hearing.

Lily pressed her lips together. "You really don't know, do you?" She sighed. "How I envied you. You spoke up. Didn't let them walk all over you. Even did your best to protect me. I'm sorry I couldn't tell you."

"Couldn't tell me what?" Rose was hurt to the quick to think Lily felt she couldn't confide in her after all they had been through together over the years.

"Our mother came to me not long ago. She told me she was grooming me for a special role. The bride of our Lord. Except the Lord had sent our father to be his proxy on earth. And I was to do whatever our father said. Give myself to him."

"Oh, my word," Rose said. "And to think I envied you the amount of time she spent with you. I felt like I ceased to exist."

"Don't worry. I didn't believe what she said. I knew it was wrong. And that I had to get away. So when we came across those strangers, despite the evil things they had done, I didn't care. To me, they represented my salvation."

"You should have told me."

"You know what *they're* like. How they try to manipulate your every thought. Our mother had me believing you knew about it and approved."

"I never—"

"I know," Lily said. "They're just so good at manipulating others. All those years of practice with the native tribes, only to turn it on their own daughters."

Rose rolled over and pulled Lily into her arms. "I'm so glad the nightmare is finally over. For both of us."

"Barron says they have a plan they need our help with."

"I don't know, Lily. I'm not sure it's such a good idea."

"He says if we do our part, it will wipe out any indebtedness to him and his brother. Even the money they paid out to Zara." Lily gave Rose's arm a playful swat. "Remember when we were younger, the plays we used to create to amuse ourselves? This won't be much different. We'll each have a role to act out."

Rose hugged her sister close and wished it was all as easy as Lily made it sound.

IF ROSE HAD FOUND Yuma a welcome sight when they reached that town, Bullet's familiar streets and buildings appeared ten times more inviting. Safe. Comforting. Welcoming. Like an old friend.

They had been mixing things up on the ride back, so that sometimes Lily rode with her, sometimes with one of the twins. Occasionally Lily rode alone and Rose rode with one or the other of the twins.

When they reached Bullet and Rose started in the direction of the café, Bishop reached out and grabbed the reins of her horse, turning her mount the other way.

"What are you doing?"

Barron and Lily watched the stand-off from a distance.

Bishop steered in close to her, one set of reins in each hand. "Going out to the ranch. What are you doing?"

"I'm not going out to the ranch," Rose said firmly. "I'm taking Lily and going to Georgina's."

"Barron and I think you girls should stay at the ranch for now."

Rose blew out a breath. "You don't trust me to stay put. I get it. But truly, Lily and I have nowhere else to go."

Bishop subjected her to a hard, long look. "That hasn't stopped you before."

"It's not my fault we never stayed in one place the whole time we were growing up."

"So maybe you don't know how to stay put."

She squared her shoulders. "Do you?"

His grin infuriated her. As if he had a secret she wasn't privy to.

"I'm trying to learn. Longer we stay here, the more natural it feels."

"I plan to try it as well. See how it feels." She pointedly reclaimed the reins and dismounted, then turned to Lily, who was deep in conversation with Barron. "You coming?"

Lily nodded her head at Barron, who dismounted and helped her down.

Bishop remained mounted. Rose suspected he liked looking down at her.

"I'll be in touch," he said finally.

"You know where to find us."

Rose stopped at the café and made sure it was okay with

Georgina if Lily shared her room at the back of the restaurant.

"Of course," Georgina said. "But there's an extra room over at the house. Wouldn't you both be more comfortable there?"

Rose shook her head. "Thank you, but the room here will do us just fine." She couldn't bear the thought of being any more indebted to Georgina than she already was.

Georgina gave her a knowing look. "Stay out back if it suits you. But for now, I'd say you look like you could use a long, hot bath. Go over to my place. Tell mother I said it was okay."

"Thank you." Rose looked over her shoulder to where Lily stood in the street, holding the reins of their horse. "We'll just take the horse to the livery first and see to him. We've had some hard days riding."

"You get cleaned up and come back over here for a hot meal, both of you," Georgina said, before she added—, "I've missed you. So have the customers."

Rose swallowed the lump in her throat. "Why are you being so kind? After I up and ran off on you without a word."

"Sometimes a body needs to do something that makes no sense to anyone but themselves. Who am I to be judging what anyone else has done?"

"You boys planning on staying put for a while?" Brody asked.

Bishop looked to Barron aware Brody directed his question to both of them. And with good reason.

"Yes, sir," Barron said.

"I got no quarrel with the two of you helping Rose to find her sister. It was the right thing to do, and any of us would have helped if we'd been asked to join in."

"We figured we had it covered," Bishop said.

"Right up until they ran off," Barron said. "But it worked out. Lily remembers stuff and is talking up a blue streak."

"What are the girls planning to do now?" Brody said.

"Rose claims they aim to stay put a spell. Help out Georgina."

"Half expected you to bring them back here," Brody said.

Bishop and Barron exchanged a look. Brody really did know them too well.

HAWKES CAME across his hired help jawing the time away when they ought to have been working. Haywire was jabbering to Denim, waving his arms around like some sort of circus performer. Both men looked up guiltily when they saw him approach.

Hawkes gave each of them a long, hard look then he took his sweet time dismounting, feeling the silence tighten like a noose around a hanged man's neck. He swaggered toward them wordlessly, enjoying seeing the look of trepidation and fear cross both their faces. He hitched his britches. Only right that folks should be a little fearful of who he was and what he might do.

"What's up, boys?"

The two men exchanged a worried look.

He let out an aggrieved sigh. "Might as well tell me. You know I'll get it out of you sooner or later."

Haywire licked his blubbery lips. "I seen her in town. With two of them Masons."

Hawkes bit back his impatience. "Who'd you see, Haywire? Spit it out."

"That lil gal. One that ... you know. Where the money come from."

"Ah," Hawkes said. "Your little side job that you originally neglected to mention to me. Somehow she managed to find her way to Bullet. Maybe she misses you?"

Haywire looked down at the ground.

"Or maybe she has coincidentally joined forces with the Masons. Is that what you think happened?"

"Dunno," Haywire said.

"Or maybe the Masons are her new champions. Planning to get even with you for accosting her." He pressed his lips together thoughtfully. "Come to think of it, that wouldn't be such a bad thing. Long as they don't know we know."

He moved to Haywire's side, pleased to see the way his flunky shrank back at Hawkes's approach. The man flinched when Hawkes clapped him on the shoulder. "Good job, Haywire. Keep your eyes and ears open and report everything back to me."

He turned to his foreman. "Pay attention to your friend here, Denim. Maybe you'll actually learn something for a change."

He turned away and mounted his horse, but not before he saw Denim's mouth tighten in displeasure.

He smiled to himself as he rode away. It was setting up to be a very good day, indeed.

~

GEORGINA BUSTLED up to Rose and Lily in the kitchen of the café. "I'll take over here, girls. You two scamper over to the hall, okay? Henrietta needs your help."

"Help with what?" Rose asked.

"I'm not sure, exactly. But Amanda's time is coming any day now, and it seems Henrietta has taken on too much. Between the hall and her other project, she could use a hand so I volunteered you two. I didn't think you'd mind."

"I didn't know Amanda's baby was due so soon," Rose said.

"She's carrying sideways, so she doesn't look all that big," Georgina said. "Doc Parsons is afraid she could have a difficult time if the baby doesn't turn soon."

Lily looked at Rose and shuddered. "I'm never having children."

Rose met her gaze. "We didn't exactly get a great example growing up of what a real family is supposed to be like. It's different out at the ranch. More the way I think family is supposed to be."

"You can have it," Lily said, as they crossed the street and headed for the hall. "I plan to be an independent business-woman like Georgina, here. Or Zara."

Rose laughed in disbelief. "You want to run a place like Zara's?"

"Not necessarily. It just must be nice not to be depen-dent on a man." Lily shot Rose a cheeky grin. "I heard the girls talking when I was at Zara's. A few of them come to Bullet a couple of nights a week. Maybe Zara needs someone to run the place for her."

Rose sniffed. "I think there are other ways to be indepen-dent and still have a family. Look at Henrietta. She's married to Braydon, but I don't think marriage has cramped her style much."

"Of course it has. Henrietta used to go to all sorts of interesting places. She's done things most women don't even dream about. She even went to Oxford University. I think she was the only woman there. Now she's stuck here in Bullet."

To Rose, being stuck in Bullet with a man you loved didn't sound like such a dreadful thing at all.

They reached the hall, where they found Henrietta in the upstairs room that served as an office. Henrietta was hunched over the desk, staring down at what looked like that same batch of papers Rose had seen the ladies perusing at the ranch.

Rose knocked on the doorframe to get Henrietta's attention.

Henrietta looked their way, but unlike last time didn't jump up and roll the papers out of sight.

"Thanks for coming, ladies." She rose and gave them both a hug, which felt strange to Rose. The only person she'd ever hugged was her sister. Other than Bishop, of course. But that was because she wanted something from him. Did Henrietta want something from them?"

Lily was staring in fascination at the papers on the desk.
"What's that?"

"Sketches for a hotel I hope to build here in town."

Rose's eyes widened. "You're building a hotel?"

"One of these days," Henrietta said. "Braydon wants me to hold off a while. Amanda ran into all sorts of problems getting this place built because of—" She stopped abruptly.

"It's okay," Rose said. "We know about Hawkes. I saw him at the christening, remember?"

"Right," Henrietta said. "I forgot you were there that day. Anyway, Braydon says we should just wait a bit on any more building projects. And with Amanda so close to her time, she needs my help here at the hall. Organizing classes and dances and activities."

Rose felt honored to be included. "How can we help?"

"When I lived in England with my grandmother, we used to have taffy pulls at the house around Halloween. Grandmadre knew a lot of people from Scotland who took Halloween really seriously." She shrugged. "The English are more into Guy Fawkes Day, but here in the territories Halloween is more popular. I thought it would be fun to do something similar in Bullet. Get the local families involved. In England we used to carve turnips, but over here it's more common to carve pumpkins."

"You carved vegetables?" Rose asked. "Why?"

"All Hallow's Eve is the last day of the month. It's believed to be a time when the barrier between this world and the spirit world thins enough so the spirits can cross over. Scary lanterns and costumes are supposed to keep any evil spirits away."

"Our father would say that was pagan," Rose said.

"It's actually based in Christianity," Henrietta said. "The same as All Saint's Day. At any rate, I thought it would be fun to do something to celebrate. I haven't had taffy in years."

"What is taffy?" Lily asked.

"I forget you girls have been basically living in the wilds," Henrietta said with a laugh. "It's a sweet candy made from boiling molasses or sugar. Grandmadre used to add rum for flavor. Once it's mixed up you pull on it so it gets soft. After that, you roll it into a rope and cut it into pieces. It's delicious."

"How do you pull it?" Rose asked. There was so much she had to learn about the world and how other folks lived.

"I'll show you when we make it. It's easy. Each person

just takes an end and pulls, which adds air bubbles. Anyway, we'll talk more about that later. For now, I suggest we go give Storm a hand in the library. I gather it's quite different from lending books out of the back of a wagon."

ROSE ROLLED over and stared into the darkness toward the ceiling of the small room in back of the café. Next to her, Lily slept peacefully. It had been a full and busy week, between helping Storm at the library and serving meals at the café. Rose felt proud that she'd already done some book lending from the wagon, so knew how to fill out and file the lending cards.

Storm had been generous with her praise and her thanks, leaving Rose to feel, for the first time in her life, that she belonged somewhere. That she not only fit in, she was a part of things. Part of a community.

Her thoughts were broken by a soft ping against the window glass. It sounded like a pebble. Careful not to disturb Lily, she climbed out of bed and went to look out, just as another pebble hit the glass. Aided by the faint light of the half moon, she could make out Bishop's familiar form a short distance away. Signaling that she'd be right out, she hastily slipped into her gown and boots and moved through the darkened café and out the front door to join him.

"Did I wake you?" The moonlight gilded his skin silver and darkened his hair in contrast. Her heart gave a hiccup at the sight of him. How had this man come to mean so much to her in such a short time?

She shook her head, her eyes never leaving his.

"I hear you're settling in. Helping Henny and Storm with stuff in town."

"That's right." She couldn't find the words to share her feelings, how right it felt to be here and be part of the goings-on. Surely he understood how she felt. How, thanks to him, she had ended up here.

"Barron and I are leaving in the morning."

"Where are you going?"

"Down to Mexico. The new herd is ready for pick up."

Why did the thought of him not being here strike such an empty chord inside her? True, she hadn't seen him lately, but she always knew he was close by.

"How long will you be gone?"

"Hard to say. A week or two, depending."

"What about the plan to ruin Hawkes? The one you need Lily and I to help you with?"

"Yeah. About that." He looked down and scuffed the dust with the toe of his boot. "That doesn't look like it's going to pan out after all."

"But Barron was telling Lily all about it. That he was getting things all set up."

"Barron talks a lot," Bishop said. "Both of us get riled up good when we think about Hawkes killing our brother. Problem is, acting out of that riled-up place is never smart. Brody knows that and reins us in. Partly why he's sending us away."

"Can't some of the others go instead? Seems like you've been away all the time lately."

Bishop blew out a breath. "Bradley's not about to go right now and leave Amanda. Not with the baby coming any day. Brody's busy with the ranch and being a dad. Blake's not too interested in leaving his new wife. Braydon is going a little crazy working the ranch and trying to help Henny at the same time. That leaves us three bachelors as the obvious pick."

Rose swallowed her disappointment. "But you'll miss the Halloween party we're planning with Henrietta." She'd been secretly looking forward to the festivities. Storm was making her and Lily costumes. Rose had never been to a party before. She'd thought it might be a chance for her and Bishop— for her and Bishop to what? Be normal? Have fun? Forget about all the bad things that had originally brought them together? Forget about schemes and deceit and vengeance?

I just want to be normal, Rose thought. Not the dutiful daughter of the crazy missionary. Not subservient. Not less of a person than everyone else. Most of all, she wanted to be with Bishop. No complications. No ulterior motives. Just the two of them. Whatever that ended up being. Friends or—

Dare she even think more?

He'd kissed her. He'd been nice to her. Surely he must like her. Even a little.

She swayed toward him, feeling wanton and willing. Bathed in silence and moonlight.

He must have realized her intentions. He raised his hands between them. "Rose, don't."

Rose, do, said her little internal voice.

"I want to." She took his hands very deliberately and placed them on her waist. She raised her hands to cup his face, loving the play of light and shadow, emphasizing the conflicting feelings playing across his handsome features.

He wanted her!

It was obvious, and when she moved half a step closer, his hands tightened possessively around her middle, pulling her even closer. Slowly they became joined. Hip to hip. Thigh to thigh. Breast to chest. And finally lips atop lips.

She was ready for him. Hungry for him. Drowning in

him and with him. His hat fell to the ground as she tangled her fingers through his hair. Her heart and soul sang at the rightness of being here. Right here. Right now. Being where she belonged.

CHAPTER 10

B ishop knew full well he shouldn't be kissing Rose out here in the moonlight. Shouldn't be flush up against her like two spoons in a drawer, while their mouths explored and celebrated each other and urgency fueled their movements.

He could feel her hands all over him, scratching his back, cupping his butt, smoothing his chest, and his skin burned through his clothing from her touch. His loins tightened as he imagined nothing between them, just the glorious sensation of skin brushing skin. Limbs softening in readiness ...

He closed his eyes in pleasure as her lips followed the questing touch of her hands. She was tonguing and nibbling his throat in a way that sent a surge of blood to his other head. The one that didn't think so good at times like this.

With the last vestige of control he was able to muster up, he wrenched himself from her embrace. His chest rose and fell as he fought for breath and pushed his hair back from his face.

She looked up at him, eyes wide and puzzled, dark red

lips damp and swollen, her tongue darting between them before she bit her bottom lip in confusion.

"What's wrong?"

What's wrong?

Nothing.

Everything.

He bent down to retrieve his hat and buy himself some time.

"That shouldn't have happened," he said finally. "Makes what I came to say even harder."

He watched her stiffen and close down right before his eyes, as if the shutters on an abandoned house had been slammed shut. "What did you come to say?"

"I came to release you from whatever obligation you feel I put on you."

"But you did what I asked. Help me find Lily. I owe you. You said as much."

He gave his head a toss, ran a hand through his hair and plopped his hat back on his head. "That's what I mean. You don't owe me anything. Not you or your sister. You're both free to go. Wherever. Whenever. Know I won't be showing up to drag you back out of some misplaced sense of being owed. Take off to whatever part of the world grabs your fancy. You needn't stick around here anymore."

Message delivered, he turned and walked away, aware of Rose's eyes following his every move as he reached his horse and swung himself into the saddle.

He couldn't stop himself from looking back once. She stood where he had left her. Hopefully, by the time he returned from Mexico she would be gone. And with her all the temptation, all the unwanted feelings she was stirring up inside him.

He had no ken with a woman complicating his life.

Especially one who looked and felt and kissed the way Rose did.

Barron and Benjamin were already up and moving about by the time he reached the ranch.

"We wondered if you up and left without us," Barron said with a level look. "Where you been?"

"No place. Just out," Bishop said shortly.

"Was she pretty?" Benjamin asked.

"Was who pretty?" Bishop snapped.

"Whoever got you all messed up. Is that a hickey?"

"Bite me!" Bishop pushed past them into his room, but not before he saw Barron and Ben exchange a knowing smirk. Inside his room, he squinted in the mirror. Sure enough, right near the base of his throat, Rose had left her mark.

"Damn woman," he muttered as he grabbed up his bedroll and headed for the barn.

The sun was just shaking itself awake as he led his horse outside to where Barron and Ben were already mounted and waiting. Before they moved one step, they heard the sound of a wagon's approach.

"What the hell!" Bishop recognized the colorful caravan of the crazy fortune-teller they'd run into up near the river-boat dock at Castle Dome Landing.

Barron recognized the caravan as well. "What's he doing here?"

"Beats me. Strikes me how he's trespassing, though."

The driver pulled his wagon to a stop nearby. "Gentle-men. We meet again."

"You guys know this joker?" Ben asked.

"Not exactly," Bishop said. "You're on private land." He raised his voice to the newcomer.

"I expect you gents might know where I can find one Brody Mason."

"Who's asking?" Ben said in a near snarl.

"That would be between Mr. Mason and I." He turned in Bishop's direction. "The sisters are reunited."

Bishop felt an uneasy twinge. "Who are you?"

"Just a simple man whose life is entwined with this family. I mean no harm," he added, over the scoffing reaction to his words.

Bishop gave the other two a skeptical look. "What do you say? Shall we run this joker back to wherever he came from?"

The man skewered Bishop with his stare. Bishop felt the look go right through him like a bullet, in one side and out the other.

"Your lady is most sad. Wounded by your words. By the idea that you care nothing for her." His dark gaze continued to bore through Bishop. "We both know that is far from the truth."

Bishop felt rather than saw Brody approach from behind.

"I'll take care of this," Brody said. "You three hit the trail as planned."

Bishop shot Brody a worried look. "You sure?"

Brody nodded. "Mr. Snake Oil and I are overdue to have a conversation."

Benjamin frowned. "What do you need to talk to this joker about?"

"If I'm not mistaken, he and I share the same mother." Brody addressed the man driving the caravan. "Isn't that what this is about?"

The man bowed his head. "I want nothing from you. I know you have a daughter." He hesitated before he spoke.

"Our mother spoke of you often. From her deathbed, she begged me to find you. To ask you to find it in your heart to forgive her. This visit fulfills my obligation."

Picking up the reins, the man turned the caravan around and headed back the way he had come.

Bishop stared, speechless, at Brody who watched the caravan's retreat, face devoid of expression.

Ben spoke up. "How did you know?"

"Same caravan my mother left in. Not something I'm likely ever to forget."

"Think we've seen the last of him?" Barron asked.

"For the time being." Brody turned and walked away.

ROSE MOVED through her days as if in a fog. Her appetite deserted her, and soon her skirt swished loosely around her waist. Georgina's attempts to fatten her up went nowhere. All she could think about was Bishop's words coming back to her.

Free to go. Whenever. Wherever.

The truth was, as much as she'd like to simply disappear, to be gone before he got back, she had no other place to go.

Oh, she could do it. Strike out someplace new and create some sort of life for herself and Lily. But Lily was thriving here in Bullet. So much so that Rose felt like they'd switched personalities. Nowadays she was the one who worked mostly in silence and spoke only when spoken to.

Lily, on the other hand, had turned into a chatter bug, her never-ending conversation full of quips and observations and enthusiasm. She'd become fast friends with Henrietta, and more often than not, Rose could find her sister at the hall, knee-deep in ideas to make the upcoming Halloween party bigger and better.

Rose didn't mind. It gave her time alone.

"Look what Henrietta and I found at the store." Lily burst into the room in a whirl of energy. "Why is it so dark in here?" She lit a candle, its weak glow casting a golden circle in part of the room. Rose blinked and looked away from the brightness.

Ignoring Rose's lack of enthusiasm, Lily unfastened the parcel and shook out the contents. "Feel how soft this is."

A bolt of light blue cloth landed on the bed next to her.

"What's that for?" Rose asked, trying to muster up a little enthusiasm.

"What is wrong with you?" Lily asked. "You've been moping around all week like you lost your best friend. But I'm right here," she added with an infectious grin. "Shake yourself off. We've been invited to the ranch."

The ranch!

"I'm not going," Rose said flatly.

"Of course, you're going. We've been invited to tea to meet Amanda's baby. It would be rude to refuse." Lily stroked the soft blue fabric. "Storm offered to sew this into a wee outfit for the baby. It's our birthing gift," she added, waving her arms in frustration at Rose's lack of enthusiasm. "I've never seen a newborn before. I can't wait."

"I think I might be coming down with something," Rose said. "You better go without me."

"Not a chance," Lily said flatly. "Georgina is going as well. She offered to pick us up and drive us. Now wash your face and brush your hair. We're going."

The ranch house was humming with female chatter when they arrived. A serene-looking Amanda occupied the place of honor in a rocking chair in one corner of the parlor, holding her new son. Across the large, open area, Rose saw Laura bustling about in the kitchen. Nearby, Storm held Laura's daughter on one hip as she laid tea things on the table. Henrietta stood at the sink washing dishes and chatting up a storm about the upcoming Halloween party at the hall.

Henrietta looked up at their arrival. "Lily. There you are. I was just telling the others about the clever Halloween posters you made to put up around town."

Rose felt a hollow thud inside her when Lily joined the others in the kitchen, as naturally as if she'd been doing it all her life. Georgina followed.

Over in the parlor, Amanda patted the chair next to her. "Come sit down, Rose. Tell me all that's been going on in town while I've been sequestered out here." She smiled as she spoke, letting Rose know hers had been a happy choice.

Because it seemed required, Rose peered at the tiny red face and thatch of dark hair barely visible from the blanket bundle in Amanda's arms. "Goodness, he's small," she said.

"You wouldn't think so if you'd been the one squeezing him out into the world," Amanda said with a laugh.

Rose blushed at the woman's plain speaking.

Amanda patted her hand. "It's okay. I had nothing to do with babies and children growing up— It was just Ma and I." She waved a hand to encompass the room and its occupants. "This has been a huge education all around. A big family. Folks always underfoot. It can take some getting used to."

Rose sighed, knowing she would never have that opportunity, to be part of a life and family like the one here at Copper Moon.

"Your sister is quite the gal," Amanda continued. "I'm

ever so grateful to her for jumping in to help Henrietta at the hall."

Rose worried her lower lip. How could she even consider leaving here and taking Lily away from a life that so agreed with her?

How could she consider staying?

"What did you name the baby?" she asked in an attempt to deflect the conversation away from her and Lily.

Amanda all but cooed. "Bradley is so thoughtful. I never knew my father since he died before I was born, but Bradley insisted we honor his memory by naming the baby after him. Samuel Mason has a nice ring, don't you think?"

Rose nodded.

Amanda leaned toward her. "The man is so smitten with his new son. You'd never know he was the most confirmed bachelor I ever had the bad luck to fall in love with."

I know what that's like, Rose thought.

"These Mason boys. None of them had it easy. But whatever heartbreak Bradley caused me along the way turned out to be worth it. Here."

Rose found the tiny bundle shoved into her arms. "Be a love and hold him a sec, would you?"

"Oh, but I—"

Her words fell on deaf ears. Amanda was already on her feet and heading toward the activity over in the kitchen.

As if sensing her inexperience, the bundle in her arms started to move, making funny snuffling sounds. Rose peered into the tiny red face. Was he unable to breathe?

She started when bright, gray-blue eyes flew open and gazed her way. Did she only imagine the lifetimes of wisdom she saw in their depths?

The baby's mouth pursed. She saw a slight white haze ringing his lips.

With no idea where the instinct came from, she leaned her face close to his and made soft cooing noises at the same time she rocked him gently in her arms. Instantly his frown disappeared, and his tiny, scrunched face relaxed.

She took a deep breath of an unfamiliar smell. Soft and soothing. A fragrance she guessed must be unique to small babies.

Samuel gave a big yawn, closed his eyes and nested against her elbow. Rose held him close and felt an overwhelming rush of emotion that must come from holding new life. Holding the future.

"You're a natural." Amanda stood behind her, observing the interplay.

"Hardly," Rose scoffed.

"Babies know when they're safe and loved," Amanda said simply, as she lowered herself back into the chair with a slight grimace. "I need to get up and move every so often. Try to get things feeling more back to normal."

Rose didn't know what to say, having never been part of an intimate female conversation before. Not even when she or her sister had bad monthlies.

"Not feeling loved was part of Bradley's problem. He was left on the steps of a church after he was born. Never held and loved and fed by his mother." Amanda sighed. "Starting life that way changes a man. Makes him hard and mistrustful of everyone. Especially females."

Rose blinked in surprise. The few times she had seen Bradley, he had looked and acted the role of the happy, doting husband, totally in love with his wife.

Amanda smiled as if reading her thoughts. "It's good now. Wonderful in fact. But it took a while to break through that brick façade. I even went so far as to buy a so-called love potion from a fortune-teller." She chuckled. "Never used it, mind, but that's how desperate I felt at the time."

"Are all the Masons like that?" Rose asked.

Amanda pursed her lips. "Brody was still hurting bad from something between him and Laura that happened years earlier. Braydon, devil-may-care as he pretends to be, grew up never knowing who his mother was. He was born at Zara's place," she added.

Rose's mouth dropped open in shock.

"Blake was an orphan as well. He and Brody were the first ones to live here at the ranch. Blake and Storm had their challenges to overcome same as the rest of us." She leaned forward conspiratorially. "I think what I'm trying to say, Rose, is don't pay any attention to whatever Bishop says. He and Barron spent the better part of their lives lying to the world. I doubt they even know how to be honest with themselves."

Rose stroked a tiny clenched fist that had worked its way free of the blanket. To her amazement, perfectly-formed, miniature fingers complete with fingernails opened, stretched, and curled around her pinkie finger.

"Why did you mention Bishop?" she asked, eyes lowered to the baby in her lap.

"I've lived in Bullet my whole life. Probably know a bit more about the brothers than anyone else in this room. Bishop bringing you here for supper that night. Agreeing to help you find your sister. Let's just say actions speak louder than words. Tells me that he cares about you more than just a little."

"He told me I was free to go. No need for me to be sticking around here any longer."

"Do you want to stay?"

KATHLEEN LAWLESS

Rose blew out a breath. "I'm not sure. Then I look at Lily. I see how much she loves it here."

"I'm not asking about Lily," Amanda said bluntly. "You're the oldest, right? Likely been seeing to your sister your entire life. From here on in, you need to be thinking about you first."

Rose met her gaze. "I'm not sure I know how to do that."

"Doesn't come easy for most of us. Far simpler to think about other folks. Lots of women transfer all their caring to their husbands and their children. Put their own needs last, same as always." She waved a hand. "Look at those ladies. And me. We love our men. But we know if we don't love ourselves first, then the menfolk get shortchanged along the way."

Rose felt her eyes start to fill. One lone tear fell onto the infant in her arms and she brushed it away before Amanda noticed. She blinked rapidly to clear her vision. Then looked up at Amanda bleakly.

"I have no idea what to do."

"Oftentimes that's best. Make it up as you go along. Plans have a way of going sideways more often than not." Amanda patted her arm and reclaimed the baby at the same time. "Trust yourself, Rose. You're a good person with a good heart. Believe that, and you'll know what to do."

A PLEASANT HOUR or more passed, spent in female chatter at the ranch. As Storm regaled them with stories of All Hallow's Eve and All Saints' Day in Ireland, Rose started to catch everyone's enthusiasm for the planned festivities at the hall.

Eventually Amanda started to yawn, the men began to

130

return home, and Georgina announced they should head back to town.

Because it was getting late, she drove the rig straight to the livery.

"Do you want us to go check in at the café?" Rose asked.

"Not necessary. I'll stop in there on my way home and make sure things went smoothly without me."

"It's on our way," Rose said, not surprised when Georgina waved her off. The café was Georgina's baby. It was only natural she'd want to check on it herself.

As Rose and Lily walked toward their room out back, arms linked, a wave of contentment rarely felt washed over Rose. She felt part of things. Part of this town. And she wasn't about to go running off. At least not now.

Abruptly Lily stiffened against her. Her chatter died mid-sentence. Rose looked around but couldn't see anything that would have her sister spooked. A couple of cowpokes ambled down the road ahead, but that was all.

Lily turned, sped up, stumbled and nearly fell in her haste.

"What is it? What's wrong?" Rose asked.

"Nothing," Lily said, too quickly.

"I know you better than that."

"It's dark. I'm sure I was mistaken."

"Mistaken about what?"

"One of those men ahead. He reminded me of the man who grabbed me up. The one who sold me to Zara."

Rose felt a cold shiver chase through her. "What would he be doing here in Bullet?"

CHAPTER 11

The ranch struck Bishop as being eerily quiet, which was saying something after their time away— nights spent in the middle of nowhere after the herd was settled and the only sound was the soft hiss of the slowly dying fire.

After he and the others delivered the new herd safely to its paddock they headed for the main house and the barn. Like the rest of the ranch, the yard was too quiet. Bishop reached for his gun, aware the other two did the same. "Where do you think everyone is?"

"Beats me," Benjamin said. "Someone ought to be around, though."

"Someone is." Bishop looked over as Bradley appeared from the doorway of the barn wiping his hands on a rag. "You missed the excitement. Amanda had the baby last week." As he spoke, Bradley's face split in the biggest shit-eating grin Bishop had ever seen. "It's a boy! I left them over at the cabin resting while I went to check on things here."

"Congratulations!" Bishop joined the others as they dismounted and gathered around the new father, clapping him on the back.

Benjamin pulled out a cigar. "I've been saving this for you."

"A boy," Barron said cockily. "Didn't think you had it in you, man."

Bradley shot him a warning look. "I wouldn't be saying that too loud around Brody. He's pretty smitten with his little girl."

"For sure. But a boy! Hunting and shooting and riding," Barron said.

Benjamin interrupted. "Any takers on a bet that Brody's daughter does all that, and better than any man?"

"You got a point," Bishop said. "Where's everybody else?"

"In town. Henrietta got some bee in her bonnet about throwing a party at the hall. Masks and games and the whole nine yards. Pretty much the entire town is expected to turn out for it."

Bishop remembered Rose talking about the party before he went away and wondered if she would be there. Or if she'd taken him at his word and made a hasty retreat from Bullet and all its bad memories.

"You guys should get cleaned up and head over," Bradley said.

"Sounds like it's more for kids," Bishop said. A distant memory surfaced, one of his few happy childhood experiences before their parents were killed. Not very original, and not any special occasion, but he and Barron used to pretend to be cowboys and Indians and run around pointing play guns made from sticks at each other. Joe used to hide out and ambush them.

Bradley laughed. "Storm left some masks at the house for you three. Benjamin can go as a gun-slinger. You two can pretend to be each other."

"In other words, be ourselves," Bishop muttered on his way inside to get cleaned up.

A self he wasn't happy with. Which made the thought of stepping into someone else's shoes sound pretty appealing. Someone who wouldn't be so dumb as to tell Rose to leave town when it was totally opposite to the way he felt.

"We ought to go," Benjamin said. "Brody and the others can use a hand keeping an eye out— in case Hawkes figures the night of the evil spirits is the perfect time to wreak havoc on the town."

Or us, Bishop thought.

"I'm with you," Barron said. "Let's get fresh horses and get going."

Following the others' lead, Bishop washed and changed quickly, aware that after ten days on the trail he didn't exactly smell like a body anyone would want to get close to.

How would he feel if Rose was there?

How would he feel if she wasn't?

ROSE READJUSTED her mask as she looked around the hall. The majority of the parents in Bullet had enthusiastically embraced the idea of a community get-together, and most of the children sported some sort of mask or simple paper costume. The promised taffy pull had been more fun than anything she remembered doing, ever. The youngsters clearly thought so too, many of them still sporting smears of taffy around their masks and mouths as they came to her corner of the room. She supervised as, one at a time, the children took turns attempting to retrieve an apple floating in a wash pan of water without using their hands.

"I can't get it," one youngster wailed as she faced Rose, her hair and face streaming with water.

"But it was a very good try." Rose passed the mask she held back to the little one and slipped an apple into the girl's pocket when no one was looking.

Along with the apples and the taffy makings, Henrietta had secured popping corn from somewhere. Outside, Blake and Braydon tended a small bonfire where the corn was being popped and the smell of the delicious snack wafted in through the wide-open doors. Rose's stomach rumbled, reminding her it had been a long time since the midday meal.

At last the apples were all gone, either won at the game or given away. Rose picked up the pan of water and took it outside to dump it before it got spilled.

"Let me give you a hand with that." She glanced up as a man stepped directly into her path and reached to take the wash pan from her hands. His voice was muffled behind the red bandanna he wore pulled up over his mouth and nose. Only his eyes were visible. Bishop's eyes.

Her heart leapt into her throat and made swallowing difficult. Did he know who she was?

With her golden hair hidden beneath the scarf she wore as part of her gypsy costume, and her face obscured by her mask, Rose felt suddenly free to be anyone she wanted to be.

"Thank you." Her own voice sounded muffled as well.

"Where do you want this dumped?"

"Over there. Away from the fire."

Behind them, inside the hall, she heard sounds of music as the piano started up. One of Amanda's music students had offered to lead a game of musical chairs for the children. So much work and planning had gone into this day, it was heartwarming to see it be such a success.

Rose had heard enough murmuring among café patrons this last week to know that for many, this was their first foray into any sort of All Hallow's Eve celebrations.

It seemed Hawkes had stopped terrorizing the towns-folk, at least temporarily, and they all welcomed the chance to build their community.

"Y'all must be new in town," she drawled, doing her best imitation of someone from the South.

His eyes smiled down at her. "Came across from the underworld, special to see you."

Rose made a quick sign of the cross for protection, as she joined in the make-believe. "I don't believe in evil spirits."

"Not all of us are evil. Some of us are here to protect you from the others who are."

Rose thought about Hawkes and his threats against the entire Mason family at little Charlotte's christening. "Not all evil doers are spirits. Some of them walk freely among us."

Her companion nodded. "Their day will come to join other evil ones in the hell fires they deserve."

Just then there was a loud popping noise from the fire, almost like a gun shot, and Rose saw how quickly Bishop reached for his weapon. He only relaxed once he realized it was just the popping corn, overloud due to several cobs that had fallen into the coals.

When it looked like he might turn to leave, Rose spoke up hastily. "You must allow me tell your fortune. In thanks for your assistance."

His brow creased, as if he was considering her offer. Finally he nodded. "Over there?"

It was the same bench they had sat on when she had first approached him at Blake and Storm's wedding.

Once they were seated side by side and turned to face each other, she took his hand in hers. It was a strong hand, heavily calloused from hard labor and times he rode without gloves. She turned it over, palm up, laid it flat in her lap and pretended to study the lines dissecting the palm.

She could feel the rapid beat of his pulse, causing hers to accelerate as well. She had no idea what a real palm reader might do or say next. She cleared her throat and faked a confidence she was far from feeling.

His wrist was roped with raised blue veins, which she traced with the tip of her finger. "Hard worker," she said.

He guffawed. "Tell me something I don't know."

She traced the lines crisscrossing his palm. "This appears to be the letter M. It could refer to your name."

"Mason does start with an M," he said, his eyes still laughing at her.

"So does marriage. Been a lot of those in the Mason family lately."

"I doubt it means you are destined to be a monk," she said primly.

He laughed aloud beneath his bandanna. "I very much doubt that also. My turn."

Her heart raced as he took her hand in his and turned it over.

"Look at that," he said. "We match."

Her palm and wrist tickled as he traced over the surface, his blunt fingers lingering while his eyes probed hers. Who knew the inside of her wrist could be so sensitive? It felt like a million soft drops of rain kissed her skin and sent waves of desire lapping through her.

At the same time, his booted foot nuzzled hers. When she made no protest, his foot crept boldly beneath the hem of her gown to slowly and deliberately caress the lower portion of her leg. Except it didn't feel like his caress ended there. Tingles that erupted beneath his touch chased upward to the juncture of her thighs and beyond.

"How's my future look to you so far?" His husky voice feathered the nerve endings running up her spine.

She cleared her throat. Tried to get back to business. "It looks most robust. As long as you are careful."

"I've been careless a time or two," he said, tightening his grip on her hand so she couldn't pull away.

She caught her breath as slowly, softly, his free hand cupped the back of her neck beneath her colorful kerchief, then tangled through her hair to her scalp. Tingles ignited into flames beneath his touch.

"Hastily spoken words. Words I didn't mean. Words that could have given someone the wrong impression. Like maybe I wish they'd leave town."

"Are you saying your words were false?"

"My words were misguided," he said. "In direct opposite of what I meant and what I wanted."

"Is it too late to recall what was said in haste?" she asked.

"You tell me. Is it?"

She reached between them and tugged down the bandanna obscuring his face. "When did you realize it was me?" she said.

"The same second I looked inside and spotted you there. I only wished I was close enough to smell you." He drew in a deep, appreciative breath. "It seemed like you must be reading my mind because suddenly there you were, right in front of me."

"I didn't see you," she said, lest he get the wrong impression and think she had deliberately come outside knowing he was there.

Gently he removed the mask from her face. "I was afraid you might be gone when I got back."

Her heart took a dive recalling her hurt. "You told me to go."

"Like I just told the fortune-teller lady, I made a mistake. And you know what?" He leaned in until his forehead rested against hers. She could feel his warm breath against her skin.

"What?" Her voice quivered. Did she really want to hear what he was about to say?

"I lied then too. I would have come after you. And I would have found you. No matter how far you ran. No matter how long it took."

"You said you wouldn't do that."

"I know. Ego speaking. I told myself I didn't want this."

"This?"

"Whatever this is between us. The scary way you fill every waking thought during the day and take over every dream I have at night."

Rose blanched. She knew exactly what he meant. The same thing happened with her.

"Do you seek a cure for what ails you?"

"I think you hold the cure."

He angled toward her as if to kiss her. Rose held her breath in anticipation.

Abruptly, the evening air rang with the sound of a single gunshot.

Bishop jumped to his feet and chased the sound around the side of the building with Rose on his heels.

Those inside must have thought it was simply more popcorn, although as they passed near the fire Rose saw Braydon and Blake spring to full alert and scatter.

Around the far side of the building, Bishop skidded to a stop. Rose followed suit, barely able to make out the shape of a man unmoving on the ground with Barron leaning over him. Lily stood nearby, both hands pressed against her mouth in shock or horror or to stop herself from crying out. Rose wasn't sure which.

Barron stood and faced them as Bishop and Rose approached. The man on the ground didn't move. Bishop nudged the victim with one toe. "Who is it?"

"Don't know," Barron said.

But Rose did. She recognized the man from a few nights ago. The one who had spooked Lily.

"Is that him?" she asked her sister quietly.

Lily just nodded, round-eyed.

Barron addressed Bishop and Rose. "I was heading to the fire when I saw Lily step outside to catch some air. Saw this fella come out of nowhere. Try to grab her up." He stared down at the unmoving form. "Made sure he didn't get a chance."

Rose moved to her sister's side and placed a protective arm around her. "You were right the other night. You thought it was him." She could feel her sister shudder.

"He said since I fetched such a hefty price the first time, he was back for another go," Lily said.

Braydon and Blake chose that moment to make an appearance, closely followed by Ben.

"Can't leave you boys alone for a minute," Braydon said.

"Trouble does love us," Barron drawled. "Guess we need to get hold of the sheriff. Let him know what happened."

"No one's seen Yates around lately." Braydon nudged the unmoving victim with the toe of his boot. "Someone will have to ride into Yuma tomorrow and alert the authorities." He looked up at Barron. "You know him?"

"Pretty sure we might have seen him around with Hawkes and some of his stooges."

Rose couldn't miss the way the others all tensed and stared into the surrounding darkness.

"Bets he didn't come here alone?" Bishop said.

"None of this makes any sense," Rose said. "He was far away from here near our parents' camp when he first grabbed up Lily. Why didn't he just take the money and leave? Why stick around?"

"Nothing involving Hawkes make sense," Bishop said. "Most of all, why he isn't long gone dead and buried these past ten years."

"We can thank Brody for that," Barron muttered.

"Thank Brody for what?"

Rose glanced up to see Brody standing a short distance away. Even in the dusk she couldn't miss the rigid set to his jaw and the anger in his eyes.

STANDING OVER THE DEAD BODY, Bishop exchanged a look with his twin. Brody had warned them once before about going vigilante after Hawkes. Yet he knew exactly how Barron felt. It was a slur on their brother's memory as long as Hawkes was still here. Ten years was too damn long a time to extract vengeance.

To say nothing of all the innocent folks who got hurt by Hawkes along the way. Maybe it was time for a family meeting. Maybe him and Barron weren't the only ones who were tired of waiting.

Brody stalked right up to them. "Am I sensing a mutiny?"

Bishop blew out a breath. Brody had done a lot for him and Barron. He was entitled to their loyalty in return. "No mutiny."

Barron mumbled something that sounded like he was in agreement.

Brody turned to Lily. "This is the man who originally kidnapped you from your family?"

She nodded.

"And now he tried it a second time. Sounds like a clear case of Barron defending you. Ben, you and Barron ride into Yuma tomorrow with the body. Let the sheriff's office there know Yates hasn't been around lately and tell them what happened here tonight. That should be the end of things."

Somehow Bishop doubted it.

Not while Hawkes was still out there.

Had the dead man been acting on Hawkes's orders?

Bishop took a step toward Rose, but saw he was too late. Barron was there ahead of him, one arm around each of the sisters, guiding them away from the sight of the dead body.

ROSE ALLOWED Barron to lead her and Lily away, back inside to the party, away from death. Surely Bishop would be along soon to find her. To finish what they had started. She smiled a secret smile, hugging herself as she recalled the way his eyes smiled into hers as he leaned in to kiss her. Sure of his welcome.

Her scalp tingled remembering the way he'd run his fingers through her hair. As if his touch managed somehow to brand her as his.

It seemed those feelings had started with his subtle moves to beguile her on their very first meeting. Feelings that intensified the night he brought Lily back to her. And reached a crescendo when he'd followed the two of them to her parents' camp.

All she knew for sure was that her world felt right when he was there, and off-balance when he wasn't.

By the time things were cleaned up and she was ready to leave, he still hadn't shown up. Rose consoled herself with the fact that something important must be keeping him away. He must be needed by his family. There could be a lot going on that she knew nothing about. If that hateful man worked for Hawkes, could Hawkes himself be far away?

She got a chill as she recalled the day of little Charlotte's christening. Was tonight another bid for Hawkes to best the Masons? She thought of Amanda and her new baby. They had stayed behind at the ranch with Bradley. What if Hawkes had taken advantage of the festivities in town? What if, even now, he had Amanda and her boy in his evil clutches? There could be a million different factors keeping Bishop from her.

"WE SHOULD LEAVE," Lily announced later that night as they got ready for bed. "As soon as we can."

"Leave what? Bullet?" Rose asked. "Why?"

"I hate Barron."

Rose put down her washing flannel and faced her sister in the mirror over the wash stand. "But Barron saved you from that horrid man. He took a life in order to defend you."

"Did he?" Lily said. "He told me later he'd been following me. Said he guessed I was up to no good when he saw me meet up with that man. Accused me of being in cahoots with Hawkes. A man I don't even know and don't want to know. I think Barron killed that other man because he knew he worked for Hawkes. I don't think it had anything to do with me."

"Lily. What are you saying?"

"I'm saying I don't trust those twins. Especially Barron."

"I'm sure there's a reasonable explanation for everything that happened tonight."

"Even Bishop taking off without so much as saying goodbye to you?"

Rose picked up the face flannel and wrung it out. Lily's words closely mirrored her own thoughts.

What *was* going on with those Masons? Particularly when it came to their lifelong sworn enemy?

CHAPTER 12

Much as Bishop intended to get back to town and finish up his conversation with Rose from the other night, he found himself stuck here on the ranch. It seemed they were always short-handed since the three of them got back. Plus, Ben and Barron had spent the better part of one full day in Yuma talking to the sheriff there.

Their conversation with Yuma's lawmakers, along with the dead body, had resulted in a group of lawmen constantly underfoot, asking endless questions about the fellow who was shot, as well as Yates. When was the last time anyone had seen Yates? And where?

Bishop also couldn't get the sight of Barron with his arm around Rose out of his mind. He still heard the low murmur of his twin's voice, reassuring Rose she had nothing to worry about.

He and Barron had shared more than a few partners over the years, in a fun and non-competitive way. Certain ladies got off on the idea of two of them at the same time. But it seemed to him, in the end, the ladies always preferred Barron over him.

HAWKES BLEW out an impatient breath when he saw who was coming down the drive. You'd think that nosy marshal would have hightailed it back to Tucson by now, 'stead of hanging around asking questions for which there were apparently no satisfactory answers.

"Going someplace, Mr. Hawkes?" the marshal asked pleasantly.

"Got business in Yuma," he said shortly. "Not that it's any of your business," he muttered under his breath.

The sharp look from the marshal told him maybe he'd muttered a little louder than he meant to.

"I have a few more questions for your man," the marshal said.

"'Fraid he's not here right now."

Denim had been acting squirrelier than ever since Haywire got himself killed. Hawkes was afraid Denim might tip off and kill someone, just to feel in control again. Last thing they needed was to have the marshal tripping over any more dead bodies. Once again, he regretted having Denim move those bones. The man knew too much about Hawkes's business, which was never a good thing.

"Do you happen to know where we can find him?"

"Took himself off for a little recreation with the ladies." Hawkes winked. "If you know what I mean."

"Any idea when he'll be back?"

"Let's see now." Hawkes squinted at the sky. He'd sent Denim off on a pretense he was needed to keep watch on an unmarked spot so far in the bush no one would ever stumble across him. "Last time he went on a bender like this, he wound up in jail for a deuce."

"And jail is where he met up with that fellow who was killed."

"That's right. Same drifter showed up a while ago looking for work. Didn't have none for him and told him that, but he hung around anyway like a homeless cur. Denim's got a soft spot that way for folks. He let the other fella bunk down in the bunk house from time to time. I didn't like it, but I got a heart. Shame when a man's down on his luck." He shrugged. "From bad luck to no luck, as they say."

"Did you know you were harboring a kidnapper in your midst?"

"Didn't know nothing about that. Now if you'll excuse me, Marshal, I'm late for my appointment."

"Of course," the marshal said.

Hawkes followed the lawman down the drive to the street, happy to see the other man start to ride in the direction of the Mason place. Let him go snoop over there for a change. In the meantime, Hawkes had a tip a certain high roller was holed up in Yuma. Maybe this time he'd have a change of luck and win back the notes the other fellow was holding. Good thing about a rich bastard like that. He wasn't pressuring Hawkes to pay him back and was plenty happy to keep extending his credit.

BISHOP WAS RIDING through the herd, checking to make sure the new arrivals all looked healthy and were gaining weight. This section of the ranch had recently been irrigated to ensure a steady supply of pastureland. But as the herd grew and the need for pastureland increased, irrigation brought its own brand of risk. They were constantly on guard against someone poisoning the water supply that ran from the river into the irrigation canals.

They'd had a scare once, a false alarm as it turned out, but the incident only served to have them double their vigilance. Especially since Hawkes had bought the neighboring ranch, which allowed him easier illicit access to the far reaches of the Copper Moon.

Convinced everything was as it should be, he had just veered off back toward the ranch house when he spotted a lone rider coming his way. Not one of them.

The rider approached as if he had all the time in the world. Bishop watched and waited. His entire body grew tense before his heart gave a happy giddy up. What was Rose doing out this way?

As she drew closer, he raised his hand in a friendly wave. She waved back as her horse daintily picked its way over to him.

"What brings you out here?" It was a lame greeting, but the best he could manage.

His blood was singing with the rightness of her mounted next to him. His eyes roved over her features, as if he was committing each gorgeous part of her face to memory. Smooth brow, cute little turned-up nose and determined jaw. Most of all, his gaze was riveted to her full red lips. Lips he ached to feel beneath his.

She wore her hair loose beneath her hat, and it flowed like liquid honey over her shoulders. "I came to say goodbye."

He felt as if she had just clipped him across the Adam's apple and left him winded. "You're leaving?" he said with a croak, once he found his voice.

She nodded. "I wanted to thank you again for helping me find Lily. She loves it here."

"You're coming back though?"

Surely she wouldn't leave her sister after all she'd gone through to find her?

"Hard to say," she said.

"Where ... Where are you going?"

"Henrietta received a letter from her friend Sir Percy. He's still in Colorado and could use a hand with some research project he's working on there."

"But what about Georgina?"

"She doesn't really need my help at the café. Not now that she has Lily. She was just being kind, the way she does."

"But ... I heard Henrietta talking about the hotel she plans to build in town. How she'd have a place there for you and your sister if you want it."

Rose shrugged. "Henrietta is generous that way as well. But the hotel is still just a bunch of drawings at this point."

"You've never even met Sir Percy. What if you two don't get on?"

"From everything Henrietta told me about him, I don't see why we wouldn't like each other just fine. At least enough to work together."

Bishop narrowed his gaze. What was Henrietta up to? Was she setting up a match between Percy and Rose?

"Kind of a dry, stuffy old Brit," he said. "Not really your type at all."

She tilted her head to one side in that adorable way she had. "Oh, really. And who would you describe as my type?"

Me!

He didn't say it out loud. He couldn't.

His throat closed right up in fear. He'd loved his folks and they'd been taken. He'd adored and admired his big brother Joe, only to see the life snuffed from him as well. He'd died a little every time Barron took on a fight when they were younger, in case this was the time his brother didn't come out all in one piece. Caring about folks just brought with it too much pain. Too much risk of losing everything. Of ending up an empty shell.

"Barron warned me this would happen," she said finally, when it became obvious he had nothing more to say.

"What about Barron?"

"He told me where to find you. And that you might not like it, but that you'd watch me ride away and not lift a finger to stop me."

He narrowed his eyes. "What were you doing talking to Barron?"

"Trying to understand you," she said. "The way I see it, who knows you better than your identical twin?"

"We're not so identical."

"He said that as well. Told me you think harder and feel deeper than he does. On account of him pushing past you and getting born first."

Bishop let out a humorless laugh. "Truth is, neither of us knows which one was born first. He only claims it was him."

She edged her horse closer. "Tell me he was wrong. Tell me you wouldn't let me leave. Not without at least trying to stop me."

He tried to look away but couldn't. Like she had his eyes lassoed to her own.

"Learned a long time ago there's not much point in trying to stop a body once their mind is made up."

She smiled at him. "You're impossible. Barron told me that also. Told me he's been the only one crazy enough to love you all these years and he's plenty tired of carrying all that responsibility on his own."

Bishop looked down at the ground. "He doesn't know what he's talking about."

"He told me you'd be all full of protests. Full of denial. Full of fear." She leaned close. "You're not your brother Barron. You're very much your own man. I saw that the very first time I saw the two of you." She raised her chin. Met his gaze straight and unblinking. "That time I stowed away and you two found me, you locked me in the back of the wagon with Barron. I think even back then you were afraid to be alone with me."

"I was never afraid of a skinny chit like you," he scoffed.

She reached out, took hold of his bandanna and pulled it up so it covered his mouth and his nose, then let fall back around his throat. "You were honest with me once, told me you didn't mean it when you told me to leave. That you'd come after me. Were you lying?"

Damn her! She was pushing him so far out of his comfort zone, he felt stripped down, naked for her and the whole world to see.

"What do you want from me, Rose?"

"A really simple thing. I want the truth."

ROSE HELD HER BREATH, waiting to see what Bishop would do. What he would say. She knew she had taken a gamble that his twin knew how he ticked. How he would react. So far everything had gone according to predictions.

She hadn't told Lily about her conversation with Barron. Lily had her own strange perceptions that she was going to have to deal with.

Rose watched Bishop closely. Saw the way his whole body was on edge. Indecision at war across his face. Would he choose fight or flight?

She held her breath. Watching and waiting.

After what seemed like forever, he blew out his breath. Reached one shaky hand her way. Cupped her jaw in his calloused palm.

There was a catch in his voice when he spoke. "I'm not sure I even recognize the truth most of the time. Not even when it's right in front of me the way you are."

She nodded, turned her face to his palm and pressed a kiss there, knowing how difficult that admission was for him to make.

"All my life, Barron's been the fighter. I always just went along. Even though I was in the background, I was always busy figuring the odds. Ready to pull him back from the brink if the odds didn't look good."

"How do the odds look now?"

He leaned so close she could feel the warmth of his breath across her face. "The fact that you're here tells me they might, for once, be in my favor. That you don't really want to go help out Percy. That maybe you'd rather stay in Bullet. Make this your permanent home."

She looked down. "I've never really had a home before. Not unless you count the back of the preaching wagon, moving from one tribe to the next."

"I had a home once when I was young. Got it burned out from underneath us. Coming here, being at the ranch always felt temporary. That Barron and I would do our part to take Hawkes down. And then we'd be off. Back up to our old ways."

"Is that what you want?"

"Just always what I figured. I pull my weight around here, but I never let myself get too invested. Always expected the day would come when it was time to pull up stakes."

"I lived like that my whole life. Strikes me this is better. I can only see one way to make it better still."

"What's that?"

"The chance to share it with someone special."

He was quiet so long she was afraid she'd lost him. That fear was stronger than need. That past hurt overrode potential happiness.

Finally, he spoke. "I want to be that guy sharing it with you. But I've got to tell you—I'm afraid." He looked down. "What if I'm no good at it?"

She knew how hard that admission was for him and was searching for the right words when he looked back up, his eyes wary, as if prepared for her to turn tail and leave.

"No one's much good at things first try," she said. "I know nothing about staying put in one place. But the way I see it, you and me together gives us a lifetime to figure things out."

Rose's heart was beating so fast, it threatened to burst clean out of her chest. But she believed if you wanted something, you went for it. Hell-bent for leather. It was the only way she knew.

"I want that," Bishop said. "I want that with you."

It wasn't easy reaching across the saddle to kiss him, but he met her more than halfway.

Rose knew as his lips met hers, so long as they were each prepared to meet the other one halfway, there was nothing they couldn't manage.

She took hold of Bishop's shoulders to keep herself balanced and let him sweep her clean off her feet. Nothing in her world had ever felt so right as right here, right now, with this man.

ROSE AND BISHOP decided on the ranch to hold their wedding. Neither of them had ever had much in the way of a real home, and the ranch symbolized that nod to their future.

It was familiar. It was home.

It was where Bishop had first brought her and where they would live together in their own snug cabin. Of a certainty, they would spend time at the big house with the others, but they also planned to spend time here alone, creating their own safe oasis away from the rest of the world.

With everyone pitching in, the new cabin was finished in record time. Blake and Benjamin even managed to bang together a makeshift platform for the ceremony, as well as for the dancing that was sure to follow.

The wedding decorations were simple. Desert flowers adorned the archway over the wood platform. Rose pressed her nose to her bouquet. Henrietta had surprised her with a clutch of roses for her to carry, each rose in a different color, the best rainbow she could ever have imagined.

She found her namesake flower even more lovely than she had imagined. The bouquet's fragrance enveloped her, sweeter than anything she had ever smelled in her life.

As the music changed, Rose looked up from the roses in time to see Lily smile over her shoulder and start forward. Rose looked past her sister, straight ahead to where Bishop stood alongside his brothers, his smile touching that special place inside her reserved for him. It was a beautiful day to step forward into her new and beautiful life.

STANDING NEXT to Rose on her sister's wedding day, Lily listened with half an ear as the reverend recited the words that would bind Rose and Bishop until death. Bride and groom looked deeply into each other's eyes as they repeated their vows. On the other side of Bishop, Barron looked her way, eyes narrowed in an unspoken message. Lily responded by looking past him as if he didn't exist.

Today was a day for celebration, a gathering of family members and loved ones such as she had never been part of before. Such a shame that Barron had to be here to ruin it.

Thanks for reading *Bishop's Bride*. You might not know how important reader reviews are, but they mean a lot. Just a short sentence saying you enjoyed the book goes a long way with new readers and puts a smile on this author's face.

Review wherever your purchased *Bishop's Bride* or on Goodreads or BookBub.

And please keep in touch

Website: KathleenLawless.com
Facebook: facebook.com/kathleenlawlessnovels
Instagram: instagram.com/kathleenflawless
TikTok: tiktok.com/@kathleenflawless

If you haven't already done so, sign up for my VIP Reader's Newsletter and be the first to hear about free books, fan-priced sales, and my new series. http://eepurl.com/bVosbI

Keep reading for a preview of Seven Brides for Seven Brothers, book 6, *Barron's Bride*.

Dear Reader

The American West in the last half of the nineteenth century offers my heroines a chance to assert their independence and also introduce them to a hero who is their match in every way. My characters have their own ideas of right and wrong, good versus evil, and deal with it on their terms. It wasn't called the Wild West for nothing. Life was about conquest, survival and persistence,

I love writing a historical genre where the reader, by the simple act of picking up the book, instantly suspends disbelief. She easily forgets about her world and her woes in a tale where no one needs to empty the dishwasher or take out the trash, and adventure lies around every corner.

As an author, it's fun to carry her away to a time and place where anything could, and often did, happen. The customs of the day and the manner of dress might be different from today's world, but people are still people. They laugh, love, hurt and heal. Celebrate and mourn. They live life large. And in the untamed wildness of the settling of the west anything can happen.

Read on for an excerpt from Book 6, *Barron's Bride*.

BARRON'S BRIDE - EXCERPT
Copyright ©2019 Kathleen Lawless

Standing next to Rose on her sister's wedding day, Lily listened with half an ear as the reverend recited the words that would bind Rose and Bishop until death. Bride and groom looked deeply into each other's eyes as they repeated their vows. On the other side of Bishop, Barron looked her way, eyes narrowed in an unspoken message. Lily responded by looking past him as if he didn't exist.

Today was a day for celebration, a gathering of family members and loved ones such as she had never been part of before. Such a shame that Barron had to be here to ruin it.

Barron glanced around the assembled guests on the Copper Moon Ranch. You'd think he'd be used to weddings by now, considering the suit he'd first bought for Brody's wedding was almost worn out. So why did he feel so uneasy standing alongside Bishop, listening to his twin pledge himself to Rose till death? Sounded like one hell of a long time to him.

Since birth, it had been him and Bishop against the world. Was he jealous? Feeling his place in his brother's life usurped by a woman?

In spite of himself he glanced over at the bride's sister Lily. There was definitely something about that female he didn't trust. Maybe now that her sister was married, Lily would up and leave town. Far better if she high-tailed it back to Yuma, or better yet some place far, far away. He knew, sure as he drew his next breath, that if Lily stuck around, she was going to raise havoc on all their lives.

Get your copy of *Barron's Bride* today or keep reading to see more books by Kathleen.

ALSO BY KATHLEEN LAWLESS

Mail Order Noelle

Chelsea's Choice

Lila: Rescue Me Mail Order Brides

Here Come the Brides Volume 1

Here Come the Brides Volume 2

Sweet Contemporary Romance

Frannie (Always a Bridesmaid)

Baxter (Last Man Standing)

Blue Sky Island

One Cinderella Spring

One Stolen Summer

One Fantasy Fall

One Wondrous Winter

Sweet Christmas Romance Novellas

Holly's Wish

No Groom at the Inn

Steamy Contemporary Romance
SECRET SEDUCTIONS

Her Untamed Cowboy - Book 1

Her Undercover Cowboy - Book 2

Her Unwilling Cowboy - Book 3

Who Needs a Cowboy! - Book 4

Intimate Strangers

Steamy Historical Romance

Taboo

Unmasked

Reckless Rogues - Box Set of the 2 Books

Romantic Suspense

Final Heat

Afterburn

Women's Fiction

Fabulous at Fifty

For a complete book list visit KathleenLawless.com

To be the first to hear about Kathleen's new releases, special fan pricing sales, and also receive a free book, sign up for her VIP Reader Newsletter at http://eepurl.com/bV0sbI

ABOUT THE AUTHOR

USA Today Bestselling Author, Kathleen Lawless, blames a misspent youth watching Rawhide, Maverick and Bonanza for her fascination with cowboys, which doesn't stop her from creating a wide variety of interests and occupations for her many alpha male heroes.

With nearly 50 published novels to her credit, she enjoys pushing the boundaries of traditional romance into historical romance, contemporary romance, romantic suspense and women's fiction.

She makes her home in the Pacific Northwest and loves to hear from her readers.

~

Sign up for Kathleen's VIP Reader Newsletter to receive updates, special giveaways and fan-priced offers. http:// eepurl.com/bVosbı

KathleenLawless.com
Goodreads | BookBub
Facebook | Instagram | TikTok